# tenkara

# tenkara

## Radically Simple, Ultralight Fly Fishing

Kevin C. Kelleher, MD
With Misako Ishimura

LYONS PRESS
Guilford, Connecticut
*An imprint of Globe Pequot Press*

Lyons Press is an imprint of Globe Pequot Press.

Project editor: David Legere
Text design: Sheryl P. Kober
Layout artist: Maggie Peterson

Illustrations by Kevin C. Kelleher unless otherwise noted.

Library of Congress Cataloging-in-Publication data is available on file.

ISBN 978-0-7627-6394-8

Printed in United States of America

10 9 8 7 6 5 4 3 2 1

# contents

# acknowledgments

Thanks first to my consultant Misako Ishimura, who transformed her love of dance into the graceful rhythms of a fly rod. Your help with translations and the history of tenkara was great, your casting insight innovative, and your laughter contagious.

Thanks to Daniel W. Galhardo, the soft-speaking fisherman turned entrepreneur who introduced tenkara to the western world. Without him, few of us would have discovered the simplicity of tenkara. Your passion for simplicity have lead the way.

And thanks to Chris Stewart for his steady enthusiasm in the promotion of tenkara. His advice has helped me and many others discover the tenkara difference.

And to my wife, who missed my presence when I was lost to writing, but knew it was important to me and that was enough. You're my number one supporter. I can't say enough, Boose.

Last of course are the publishers and editors, especially Allen Jones, who saw something in this book and helped it along with professionalism, while letting a country doc rattle on about simplicity in a complex time. At the end of the day, helping to mold ideas into something a little more lasting is a very important job.

There has never before been a book about tenkara in English. Given its history is obscure, its instruction untranslated, and its practice new to our streams, there are bound to be errors or omissions. They are my responsibility. I am, after all, just a mediocre angler, a pretty good GP, and an enthusiastic outdoorsman, trying to get out a message. I have tried my best to be accurate but at some point you need to call it done and JUST GO FISHIN'.

# introduction: why tenkara?

I love being outdoors. I love leaving the noise, distractions, and strains of modern life to cast a fly. I love the grace of the cast, the quiet way a fly lands, the drift of the fly on current and eddy. Even more, I love the cold mountain streams that are best fished with a fly.

But I confess that western-style fly fishing has been a struggle at times, even after more than a decade of study. It seems that too often I end up with a tangle of line, a clanking vest of doodads, and disquieting experiences to match. It takes me twenty minutes to rig up, and then I snag my line on the way to the stream. When my cast goes haywire it is anything but graceful. I forget to watch my backcast and grow frustrated with an unnatural fly presentation, made worse by the splash of an unwieldy and weighted fly line. Western fly fishing is hard to teach too, and many refuse its complications. As I get older, my wading is not as steady, and I can't see a tiny fly much beyond twenty-five feet, especially

when the sun gets low. I've been occasionally faced with my self-imposed dictum . . . that I'll quit anything that consistently gives me a headache or makes me cuss.

But I keep coming back because of the unquestionably great days, the ones when you arrive at an empty pull-off and have the stream to yourself. Your pace is relaxed and quiet. Your cast is soft and on target. You're unhurried, relaxed, and yet, at the same time intensely focused, absorbed.

Then there is the excitement as a fish takes this daintiest of offerings, this sleight-of-hand made of fur and feather. Each sparkling fish you release is a bond to wildness. And as the sun climbs high, you can sit on a grassy bank and share a fish story with an old friend. I want more of those days. I need them.

I'm a country doctor by trade, and I've got to tell you, I think we all need more of those days. It seems to me that too many people are agitated and angry lately. They can't sleep, they eat too much, and they look for adventure on TV. People need the respite of the woods and stream, but they don't need the complications of a gear-laden expedition. They need to leave behind the burdens, not carry them. They need quiet and ease.

That's where tenkara comes in. Without a reel, and with the line hitched directly to the end of a long rod, it has an elemental simplicity, yet it can turn over a cast of such grace that it nearly guarantees a light and effective presentation.

Casting is so simple it is nearly intuitive, and can be learned in minutes. Tenkara is perfect for beginning fly anglers of any age, yet the accomplished fly angler will appreciate its accuracy and versatility, even while being presented with the familiar challenges of fly fishing. With its lightweight and telescoping storage, you can carry your entire kit in one hand. The gear is so stripped down that there is never a reason to leave your rod behind. Since there is little rigging up (there are no guides to thread, and a fly can remain attached), you can literally go from pants pocket to pocket water in less than a minute. The traditional line resists tangles and will last at least a season. You only need one spool of tippet, and most tenkara anglers fish effectively with a handful of flies. With a tenkara rod you'll fish one-handed, with your other hand available for steadying yourself, shading your eyes, or warming in a mitten. With its short but delicate reach you can always see your fly and keep your line quietly off the current; you can fish eddies that were nearly unfishable before. Preventing line drag is effortless. Bottom line? With this simple and effective rod you spend more time fishing and less time fumbling with your gear.

Fishing is not all about easy, though; fishing is about the competition, too—who can get the most, the biggest of the day, and ultimately whose stream craft is the best. It's about the need for one more cast as the light fades. It is the desire to get on the stream before the other guy or gal, and still be there when they are throwing their waders in the truck bed. But mostly the competition is with ourselves. Do I have the skills to stalk my prey? Do I have the tenacity and touch to bring him to net? The water tests us and the grading is fair.

Tenkara adds to the test. When your reach is limited, it requires a bit more stealth and planning than western fly fishing. It takes more skill to land a bigger fish on a small tippet and without a reel. It is more like hunting with a bow than a rifle. Yet done well, tenkara outfishes all other styles on small trout water. Period.

And finally, tenkara minimizes distractions. Its quietness and simplicity lets nature whisper to you in a still, soft voice. It reminds us of nature's cycles and humbles us into insignificance. It is, as tenkara expert and consultant for this book Misako Ishimura says, "a direct connection."

For me, tenkara has quieted the clatter of distractions. I've gotten rid of the extraneous and kept the essential. I fit the environment. I'm more focused and I fish better, both with my tenkara rod and my old Orvis.

Yet tenkara is not particularly serious; it has allowed the little kid in me to come out and play again. Indeed, one of the purposes of this book is to encourage you to have fun while exploring tenkara.

When I came across tenkara, I immediately saw that it encapsulated the reliability of gear and the simplicity of use that I favor in outdoor equipment and techniques. In almost forty-five years of outdoor experiences, the tweaking of my kit has constantly evolved toward simplicity. Tenkara doesn't interfere with my fun or my relaxation on the stream, and with little effort I can find contentment. As a physician I know the importance of contentment and why relaxation and quiet are important to maintaining health. It's important to me that you have a chance to experience this ease too. That's ultimately why I wrote this book.

Though it is written so complete beginners can start from scratch, seasoned fly anglers will also find all the information they need to make the transition from western to tenkara fishing. The tenkara knots, approach, and even casts are just simplified versions of the sport you already enjoy. But it's the simplicity that's going to win you over. Tenkara has everything you love about fly fishing, but with a liberating minimalism.

In a nutshell, I am writing to encourage men and women who love the outdoors to give tenkara a try. If this book helps any angler anywhere have one perfect, unencumbered day on the stream . . . well it just doesn't get any better than that.

# CHAPTER 1

# the roots of tenkara

THE HISTORY OF THE WORLD IS THE RECORD OF A MAN IN QUEST OF
HIS DAILY BREAD.

—Hedrick Wilhelm van Loon

**Tenkara has its roots in the mountains of Japan,** in the practical approach of the subsistence fisherman, and the pared-down efficiency of the professional. It is on Japan's high-gradient streams, where clear plunge pools and fast riffles place a premium on accurate presentation, that tenkara has been refined for over three centuries.

The fly rod in Japan, like its European counterpart, was designed to extend the reach of the angler. Because of the heavy, unwieldy wood used in the European rods, the development of the reel was likely inevitable. But the Japanese rodmaker had access to lightweight bamboo, which was used to produce lithe and aesthetically pleasing rods. Constructed in the round, they could be made in sections, allowing for easy storage and transport. There was no need for the click and whirl of the reel, nor for the excess line to go with it.

During Japan's 260-year Edo period (1603–1868), the Tokugawa shogun ensured the region's security and peace through an iron rule. With this peace came leisure, especially for the samurai. These warriors, a significant portion of the populace, were encouraged to fish. Some say this was to temper their warlike nature; others say it was to keep them fit and trained in stealth, agility, and quick reactions. The samurai, who were the dominant class, made fishing fashionable and commissioned rods from bamboo crafters. After the Meiji reforms and abolition of the feudal system, fishing became widespread, and many swordsmiths found employment crafting rods with metal fittings and even inlaid mother of pearl.[1]

In Japan there are forty-six genera of bamboo and over six hundred species. This variety allowed early rods to be joined in matched sections at the bamboo nodes. They were beautifully lacquered and strengthened with silk thread,[2] and the bamboo core was carefully removed to lighten the rods.

The art of fishing for the small, flavorful Japanese ayu was called *tengara* or *tenkara,* and consisted of two styles of fishing: silk lines rigged with a line of bare hooks or with a cast of simple flies. These long ayu rods were jigged up and down in a playful fashion from shoreline. The water fished was typically flat. In fact, this water provided the modern name for this form of fishing, *dobutsuri,* which means "fishing in slow current."

The manufacturers of sewing needles began crafting stylish flies for the court nobility and aristocrats in Kyoto. The flies, known as *kebari,* soon became a form of high art, utilizing silk in every color, dubbing "fleece" from the flowering fern, pheasant, and peacock feathers, and even gold foil. Most of these flies display a unique directional angling of the feather, the reverse hackle, and were tied on needles as small as three-eighths of an inch long . . . miniature beauty.

The first flies were likely sold in the 1600s. The Meboso family in Kanasawa and the Katsuoka family in Hyogo Prefecture have preserved this traditional craft to this day. By 1703 gold foil was being used in flies manufactured for the ugui, a small freshwater fish. In 1850 these flies were being built in Bansyu, Kaga, Tosa, and Akita for the ayu fishermen. According to Yugi Meboso, by 1926 production had reached over one million flies per year. Ninety percent of ayu flies are now manufactured in Hyogo Prefecture. The flies are tied on special eyeless and barbless hooks in a technique that takes five years to apprentice. Modern variants include such exotic materials as gold lamé and snakeskin. There are more than six hundred traditional ayu flies, many being identified with a particular geographic area such as Kaga Kebari and Bansyu Kebari.

It is interesting to note that Izaak Walton, with his "light one-handed rod," was writing *The Compleat Angler* on the other side of the world about the same time that ayu and ugui flies were being sold in Kyoto. In Spain, fishing the long rod using horsehair-furled lines with reverse hackle flies probably dates from the same era.[3] Perhaps even the long rod of the Italian Po River region dates from this time. The long rod is perhaps a natural development, but the reverse hackle fly makes for a remarkable synchrony.

The urban and coastal city dwellers would occasionally travel to the scattered mountain villages to visit the markets; they would also make pilgrimages to the Buddhist and Shugendo temples that dotted these sacred mountains. These visitors were more educated than the mountain dwellers, and their appreciation of the artistic and the aesthetic were developed to a high degree. The mountain people, by contrast, lived within the practicality of spare living and rhythm of the seasons. Travel was difficult and the mountain culture was isolated to a large degree by geography, but the mixing of the two very different cultures occurred from time to time and they influenced each other.

In this sporadic interaction, it is believed that knowledge of fishing with long bamboo rods and beautiful flies was transformed into what we now know as tenkara. This theory is supported by the general uniformity of the Japanese kebari fly and perhaps to a lesser degree by the evolution of the bamboo rod. Certainly the professional fisherman found an opportunity to supply visitors with fish at the scattered mountain inns. In any case, it is certain that tenkara as we know it today was developed primarily by the subsistence and professional fishermen who lived in the heavily forested mountains, and who fished with a focus on efficiency.

The rushing streams and shallow streambeds of mountainous Japan made the terminal sinker of the lowland rig useless. A brace of flies was also unnecessary for the rapidfire mountain casting required to harvest fish from these streams. Of course, the fishermen of the mountains could not afford the dainty and expensive flies of Kaga and Kyoto, and bait fishing made for twice the work of a reusable fly. Hence these pragmatists simplified, making the kebari fly out of only two materials, fiber and feather. With its reverse feather hackle animating the fly on quick retrieves, it was perfectly matched to the brisk mountain streams, as was noted in this nineteenth-century comparison of the Japanese fly to the British Soft Hackle by observer George Elliott Gregory:

> I am told that European flies do not succeed in Japanese rivers and had heard as a reason, assigned by a gentleman, himself an angler, that the feathers of which the wings [sic. hackles] are made, being too soft and pliant to resist the press of the rapid streams of this country, collapse and then cause the artificial fly to lose all similitude to the real insect. This would seem to be the case inasmuch as the wing of the Japanese flies are made of bristles and give to them, when out of the water, a very rough and rigid appearance as compared with that presented by flies of European make.[4]

Lines of furled horsehair replaced expensive silk even while simple bamboo rods made of a single length of bamboo were being carried over the shoulders of the mountain fishermen. Tenkara fishing became a reliable source of food. Any excess fish were sold in the markets. Though the ayu was not available to the mountain fisherman, other fish were. The *iwana,* which means "fish of the rocks," is actually a char similar to our brook trout and lives in the very cold high streams. The *amago,* which means "fish in the rain" (for that is when they are best caught), and the *yamame,* which means "woman in the mountains" for its beauty, are true trout. They became market staples of the commercial fishermen.

The first known description of tenkara fishing in English is likely a report by Gregory to the Asiatic Society of Japan on March 28, 1877. This British observer described the *ke bari* fly rod as being "a simple bamboo rod," noting that "the line is used with a float but without any sink and the bait as the name *ke* implies, is an artificial fly."[5] The rod was described as being intermediate in length between the twenty-one-foot *koi-tsuri-sao* and the three-foot-six-inch *haze sao,* and was said to be used exclusively in high-gradient mountain streams. Another record of the tenkara style of fishing comes to us in the *Tateyama Mountain Climbing Diary* of Ernest M Sato (n. Sorbian), recorded in the next year. He and his companion fished in the mountains for their iwana supper. Sato was an able linguist and British diplomat during the early modernization of Japan and founded the Asiatic Society that provides our best English-language records of tenkara to this day.

While the verifiable origins of the name tenkara are likely lost, one theory has it that an early writer observed the mountain style of fishing and mis-named it for its lowland cousin. Some say the name derives from a skipping game, *chingara,* and refers to the tenkara angler jumping from rock to rock. Another proposes the name comes from *tegara,* the ancient Japanese dia-lectic for a yellow butterfly.[6] It is perhaps fitting that the name tenkara, which means "from the heavens," remains a mountain mystery.

According to one author, the modern resurgence of tenkara began in the 1920s.[7] Within thirty years a 1950 booklet described fishing with a rather stiff, twelve-foot rod, using either gelatin-coated silk line or nylon, of a length equal to the rod. Multiple sections of bamboo were also becoming the norm around this time, with some segments hollowed and used for nesting storage.[8] So effective was this rod design that it survives nearly unchanged today. We can interpret all the essentials of modern tenkara, for example, in this postwar description of tenkara from a Japa-nese tourist bureau publication:

> Silk of three threads thickness (3 rin) used as tippet leading to a feathered hook. A probable hide-out of the yamame is chosen, and there a fly is cast up-stream. Then the line is pulled toward the angler in such a manner that the feathered hook beats the surface. Yamame watches the feathered hook, and jumps at it in a flashing movement.[9]

Tenkara has persisted by providing food for the mountain people as well as mountain refugees from war and urban poverty. During the period of postwar modernization, however, tenkara's popularity plummeted, and it was not until the 1980s that it began to see a slowly expanding interest. The first small tenkara summit took place in Japan in 1993. Organized by Dr. Hisao Ishigaki, a tenkara master who has sparked much interest with his writing and videos, the 2009 summit was attended by 160 tenkara anglers. Tenkara in Japan is benefiting from a renewed interest in outdoor adventure, the historical study of the mountain regions, and nascent but expanding catch and release practices.

In the United States, interest has been stirred in part thanks to a presentation of tenkara at the Catskills Fly-fishing Center and Museum on May 23, 2009. Accompanying the exhibit of Japanese fly-fishing materials ("Made in Japan" was coordinated by my consultant Misako Ishimura and will become part of their international collection), the tenkara demonstration was attended by fly-fishing legend Joan Wulff, who is a director at the center. Dr. Ishigaki came from Japan to provide American anglers with the rare opportunity to see tenkara firsthand, donating flies, rods, and lines to the exhibit. He provided a lecture and streamside presentation of tenkara casting, emphasizing that fly fishing could be made simple and uncomplicated, and advocating for catch and release. His emphasis on the unfussy extends to the simple, two-material fly he ties with hen hackle and sewing thread. He backs his provocative, pared-down, one-fly fishing techniques with science. A doctor of medicine and professor of visual training, Dr. Ishigaki has studied the visual acuity and peripheral vision of the trout (as well as professional athletes and sportsmen), contending that the motion and presentation of the fly far exceeds the blurred image recorded by trout acuity.

Serendipitously, in the month before the show opened, the tenkara rod was introduced to the Western Hemisphere through the enthusiasm and vision of then twenty-seven-year-old Daniel W. Galhardo. His company, Tenkara USA, has almost singlehandedly introduced tenkara to the western world, and has made extensive tenkara information available on its Web site. Complementing his work, the debate among fly-fishing forums and the curiosity of the major fly-fishing magazines has also been instrumental in the mounting interest in tenkara. Especially popular with hikers and ultralight backpackers, interest in tenkara has been phenomenal.

Tenkara is spreading internationally too. New Zealanders and Aussies are finding tenkara effective on their ultraclear streams even while the Italians are adapting to tenkara in the fast streams of Valsesia in northern Italy. The Swiss are fishing tenkara, and it's being taken up by anglers in England and Wales, where the similarities between the traditional North Country Yorkshire fly and the traditional Japanese kebari fly have no doubt been noted.

Meanwhile, tenkara in the United States is already evolving. The centuries-old kebari fly and its traditional staccato stream presentation are being supplanted and extended by the many varieties of flies and fishing styles that characterize American fly fishing. This adaptation of tenkara is inevitable, although I hope that the origins of tenkara, from the hands of the pragmatic mountain fisherman, will not be forgotten.

## Sources from Pages 1-7

1. Matuzaki, Meizi, *Angling in Japan,* Board of Tourist Industry Japanese Government Railways, 1940, p. 14.
2. Ibid., p. 12.
3. Basurto, Fernado, *The Little Treatise on Fishing,* 1539. Juan de Berga, *Manuscrito de Astorga,* 1624.
4. Gregory, George Elliott, "Japanese Fisheries" in the *Transactions of the Asiatic Society of Japan,* vol. v, part I, March 28, 1877, p. 103 footnote.
5. Ibid., pp. 103–4.
6. Seseki, Yamamoto, www1.bbiq.jp/yamame/gogen_tenkara.htm.
7. Takeuchi, Junsaburo, *Modern Angling in Japan,* Shiryosha, Tokyo, 1950.
8. Sato, Koseki, *Japanese Angler,* Foreign Affairs Association of Japan, Tokyo, undated but est. 1955, pp. 10–11.
9. Ibid., pp. 16–17.

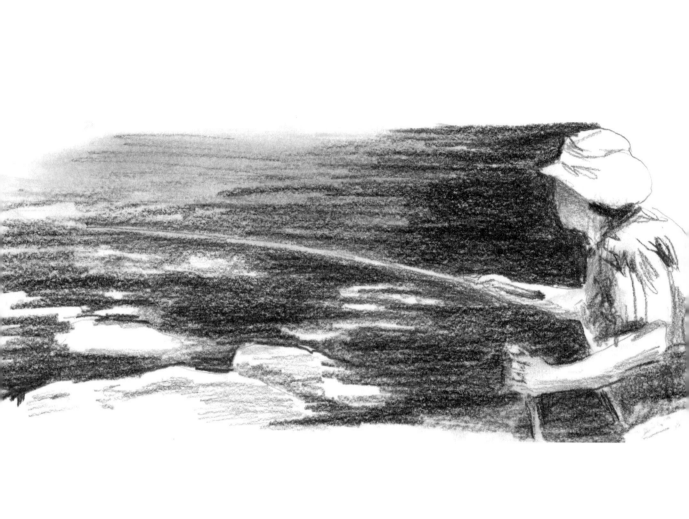

# CHAPTER 2

# gear simplicity

ONLY BY GOING ALONE IN SILENCE, WITHOUT LUGGAGE, CAN ONE
TRULY GET INTO THE HEART OF THE WILDERNESS.

—John Muir

The principal appeal of tenkara fly fishing lies in its simplicity, pared down to a rod, a line, and a fly. In comparison to western fly fishing, the amount of necessary gear is minimal. The small amount of gear you do decide to carry should reflect the water you fish, your inventiveness, and your comfort level. Take only what seems essential and fitting. Scrutinize everything. It must serve you, not burden you.

## the tenkara rod

Modern tenkara rods are technological wonders. Carbon-reinforced polymers have revolutionized tenkara. These rods are amazingly light, have a high strength-to-weight ratio, and have a telescoping package that allows for compact storage. Modern tenkara rods typically weigh two to four ounces, and are generally nine to fifteen feet long, with as many as eleven sections. The handle or grip contains the telescoping sections, allowing for easy transport. The remarkable collapsed package is only fourteen to twenty-four inches long, perfect for carry-on luggage or an ultralight backpack.

There are a surprising number of telescoping rods in Japan, each aimed at a specific type of fishing. However, a tenkara rod by definition has a grip, and its length is effectively limited to fifteen feet or less. The grip and length limitation are necessary to provide a light, balanced rod, which is comfortable for the repeated casting needed for all-day fly pre-sentation. Great care is taken to properly balance a tenkara rod.

Since tenkara rods have no reels, the line is attached at the tip. This may remind you of a cane pole, and, in many ways, a tenkara rod does reflect the cane pole's simplicity. The grace and delicate presentation of the tenkara rod, however, supplied by its smooth application of power, far exceeds the cane pole or its poor cousins, the crappie pole and loop rod. The hollow, refined carbon modular components allow a transfer of force through the rod's long lever arm, resulting in an almost effortless turning over of the line and fly. The rod actually becomes part of the flexing compound curve that turns over the line. Its tip, in the range of three hundredths of an inch (0.03"), is so flexible it becomes part of the cast. Indeed I have often said that the tenkara rod simply "launches a leader," rather than a line.

Tenkara rods are rated by a ratio based on the number of stiff to supple sections. For instance, a 6:4 rod has six stiffer sections combined with four more flexible ones: the larger the ratio, the stiffer, or "faster," the rod. When you "shake test" a tenkara rod, this ratio will predict the point of maximum flex. But keep in mind that the tenkara rod, particularly because of its length, is slower than traditional fly rods. This makes it ideal for short and delicate presentations.

A standardized method of describing a fly rod's action in its entirety has not yet been devised. The "Common Cents System"[1] is perhaps the most useful. When you choose your rod, remember that tenkara rods do not describe the same kind of compound curve as do fly rods. The so-called "action angle" is of little use in describing their speed. More useful, the ERN (Effective Rod Number) values that correspond to the weight of line in the western system roughly correlate with the "stiffness" of the tenkara rod. Measurements of a sampling of tenkara rods correspond with western rods, from a one-weight all the way to a six-weight rod. I prefer rods at the softer (lower) end for their ease in casting. A stiffer (higher) rod has the ability to manage larger fish but tends to need a bit more muscle in casting. For now, test casting a tenkara rod is the best way to match your particular sensibilities and style.

One particularly ingenious innovation of the modern tenkara rod is in its telescoping grip storage. This compact storage makes for one of the smallest packages in fishing even while creating one of the longest reaches. With a simple unscrewing of the butt cap, all the pieces can be removed for cleaning and easily and inexpensively replaced if damaged. When extending or collapsing your tenkara rod, be sure to push and pull *in-line* with the long axis; most damage occurs when collapsing the rod. Make sure the sections are snug, ensuring a smooth action, but don't over tighten. Cleaning your rod from time to time with a soft cloth and drying it after a day on the stream is always a good idea, and can make for a nice, mindful conclusion to a fishing excursion. Gear readiness also makes your next spontaneous outing more likely. Lightly waxing the joining sections can aid the fit, making telescoping in freezing weather easier.

Tenkara rod grips are made from cork, wood, or foam. Wooden handles weigh the most, though some anglers like their balance or claim they transmit vibration better. Generally speaking, traditional cork is more practical, lighter, and causes less chafing. I prefer it. Foam is light and the least expensive, but can cause significantly more hand friction during a long day of fishing. Grip length is a personal preference, though longer grips allow some adjustment for near and far casting.

Carbon fiber naturally has a matte finish, though a glossy coating can be more attractive. It is doubtful that the reflectivity of such a coating spooks fish, although waving anything repeatedly above a fish will, of course, send it running for cover. Carbon fiber is an excellent conductor of electricity, so be careful around power lines and be aware of lightning risk. In an electrical storm, collapse and drop your rod. Carbon fiber will burn too, so never attempt to loosen frozen sections with a flame.

The tip of a tenkara rod has an epoxy-secured, braided line called a *lilian.*[2] The line is attached to this line with a simple hitch, which transfers the energy of the cast with efficiency and grace. The lilian is traditionally red for visibility and is simply glued in place.

Tenkara rods may be the ideal fishing rod for a beginner of any age. With its ultralight weight, a tenkara rod is easily managed by even the smallest hands. In the absence of a reel, line handling is simplified, and having only a length of line a little longer than rod length decreases snags and tangles. Single de-barbed fishhooks are safer than trebled hooks, and with the feather-light fly, tenkara packs less of a punch than gear-heavy lure fishing. A light, stealthy fly presentation is almost guaranteed by a furled line setup. Lastly, tenkara rods are perhaps the most intuitive method of fishing with a rod. One naturally hooks and lands with a simple lift of the rod. The ease of ten-kara rods have made them especially valuable to youth fly-fishing, scouting, and disabled veterans programs for the same reasons.

Given the simplicity of this gear, learning is intuitive and simple. The gear does not get in the way of the more important education: stream craft and the connection to nature. The productivity of tenkara encourages early success, and simplicity makes sure it is fun. By contrast, the learning curve of western fly fishing can be discouragingly steep. With tenkara a beginner can start on the water.

### line and tippet

The tenkara fly line consists of only two parts: line and tippet. Depending on the needs of the stream and personal preference, a fisherman can modify several different elements in this basic combination.

Simply fishing a fluorocarbon line, like regular spinning line, works well, especially when fishing under the surface. It is inexpensive and easily obtained. Fluorocarbon line, because of its density, may allow for longer casts, since the line is less susceptible to deflection and less prone to straying in the wind. A ten- to eighteen-pound test line (diameter of .011 to .016 inches) is generally preferred, depending on the wind and water conditions. Ten-pound test is usually only suitable for light air, but does allow for a delicate presentation; a fifteen-pound test is a good compromise. When the diameter of the line is the same and not tapered, it is called a level line. One advantage of using a level line is that the length can be adjusted easily on the stream, shortening it for easier casting on brushy streams or lengthening it for a greater reach on clearer water.

Fluorocarbon, with its low refractive index, becomes almost invisible in water, which means fewer spooked fish. Tenkara fluorocarbon lines often have some tint, which aids in seeing your line when casting and seems not to greatly affect its underwater appearance. As we will see, tenkara is usually fished with most of the line off the water, and the thinner fluorocarbon diameter helps the rod in keeping the line high. In this case tint can be very helpful in detecting strikes. Fluorocarbon's stiffness and density is also an asset, and is needed to cast easily.

Fluorocarbon can also be tapered in steps from thick to thinner, exactly like western fly lines and with similar characteristics. Indeed combining a stiff butt with a machine-tapered fluorocarbon line works quite well.

A few anglers combine a fluorocarbon line with a nylon intermediate section to allow for easy casting, yet some float. More commonly, a small section of brightly tinted nylon can be used as an indicator. Nylon monofilament[3] as the sole level line, however, makes a poor substitute, with its coil memory keeping it from lying straight and low density making it harder to cast.

Many tenkara fishermen, however, prefer a tapered line of the furled or braided type, usually made from monofilament, synthetic thread, or fluorocarbon. Furled lines are made by twisting small fibers together like a double-braided rope. The number of small fibers can be adjusted and tapered with great precision. Furled lines have several advantages, and should be especially appealing to beginners. First, furled lines retain little memory, casting and transferring energy more smoothly than fluorocarbon. Lack of coiling allows a limper drop onto the water, and the air resistance of the furled lines almost guarantees that a fly will land lightly rather than splashing. Second, a furled line resists tangles and tailing knots better than fluorocarbon. For the beginner, untangling a bird's nest of line is certainly a lesson in patience, though has little else to recommend it.

Furled lines are also more durable than fluorocarbon level lines and with care can last several seasons. They have a slightly higher cost, however, and perhaps higher visibility, though the latter seems to make little difference once you add several feet of tippet (the final section of very light monofilament to which the hook is knotted). The cost is certainly offset by its durability.

Some complain of line spray from a furled line, but this usually occurs only on a backcast. Of course, this is completely remedied with a false cast away from the fish. In reality though, line spray is not much of a problem with furled lines, and frankly, not much different from that which occurs with a level line.

Furled lines, because of their multi-thread composition, can spring back into a kinked tangle after pulling very hard against a tree-snagged fly. It looks worse than it is though, and can simply be "combed out" in less than a minute, simply by working your fingers down the length of the line.

Making furled lines is not difficult and allows you to control taper, weight, length, and color, as well as sink and floatability. It is also a way to save a few dollars if you have the time. (The making of single filament and furled lines will be discussed later.)

Though both level lines and furled lines have their fans, many tenkara anglers carry both. They use a level line if they need a longer cast or are fishing in windy conditions. They use furled lines if a more delicate approach is needed or if fishing in shallow streams. Because a simple hitch, easily released, is used to attach both, changing lines is simple and quick. When I teach, for instance, rather than waste time unsnarling a more complicated tangle, it is quite easy to quickly change lines and save the untangling for later.

A few tenkara fishermen use a floating, PVC-coated running line of the type made for western fly rods. The PVC line weight aids casting and the plastic coating releases easily from grassy streamside conditions. Even with the smallest diameters and weight, however, it is an easy line for fish to see, and the splash and visibility essentially sacrifice the advantage of tenkara's soft presentation. The typical tenkara furled-line weight, by comparison, is about half the weight of a 000 fly line. Experimentation has also been done with mixed material furled lines, but the fluorocarbon level line and simple furled line remain preferred.

Attached to the business end of the line, as mentioned, will be your tippet. Tippet stealth becomes very important since the fly is attached directly to it. Use a light tippet to protect your tenkara rod, based on the manufacturer's recommendations. With your increased ability to "nose" the fish, or control him, you may be surprised at how large a fish you can land on a tenkara rod and light tippet. The rod's suppleness and length adds shock protection as well. Though rod flexibility does slow your hook set slightly, this is counterbalanced by increased sensitivity. In practice, quick hooking seems to be little trouble.

Tippet can be made of nylon or fluorocarbon, the latter being less visible and sinking more quickly, and the former stretching more and giving better shock protection. It is perhaps telling that most competitive anglers favor fluorocarbon for its stealth. If you fish mostly dry flies, however, a nylon tippet is less expensive, floats better, and is kinder to the environment. Please dispose of tippet scraps properly. As they say, "mind your mono." Even biodegradable tippet may pose a wildlife danger for up to five years, while nylon lasts for much longer and fluorocarbon nearly forever.

Replace any tippet or line that is excessively worn and check your tippet for nicks after landing a fish, especially when playing it over rough streambeds and snags. If in doubt, replace it. Nylon is susceptible to ultraviolet degradation, so don't store tippet in a sunny spot and replace your supply of nylon tippet each season. Fluorocarbon can safely be used for several seasons.

Tippet can be stored on the spool on which it is purchased. Rarely will you need more than one or two sizes, 5X to 7X being the most popular. Smaller flies and clear water conditions require the finer 7X tippet, while larger flies and fish favor larger diameter tippet.

When you are fishing frequently or are simply moving from one spot to another, leave your line and tippet attached to the lilian. Partially or fully collapsing your tenkara rod allows easier walking through brush and can be accomplished quickly without re-rigging. Keep in mind though that a partially collapsed rod is susceptible to breakage; if in very brushy conditions, collapse the rod completely.

When moving, simply wind the line around a tippet spool with the fly still attached. Then by simply extending the rod as you unwind the spool, you can go from the collapsed and protected rod to fishing in less than a minute. The spool can be stored on the rod by placing it over the collapsed shaft and snugging its center hole against the cork grip. This is the traditional way to carry it in Japan.

Instead of a spool, tenkara fishermen often wind their line on a "cast holder." A cast holder was a traditional wooden holder in Europe and the colonies; the hook and line were wound in readiness for adding to a fly line or simply fishing by hand. A cast holder for a tenkara rod can be made out of a stiff piece of plastic, closed-cell foam, or light wood, anything around which the line can be wound. A groove in each end captures the point hook and the line windings. Commercial snelled-hook and dropper rig holders work too. Dropper rigs often come in a handy box, allow-

ing you to keep a couple level lines and furled lines loaded and ready for quick changes.

The slight advantage of a cast holder over a spool when backpacking is that it can be slid, along with the rod, into a protective tube, such as the rod storage tube, a plastic mailing tube, or fluorescent light tube, protecting both line and rod from brush and snags. When hiking, I lash such a mailing tube to my trekking pole, which keeps the rod handy without interfering with the trekking pole's function, even in the tightest brush.

The best solution I have found is to attach two removable hook keepers on the first part of the rod shaft. These keepers are easily attached with strong rubber O-rings, with which they are supplied. If you face them in opposing directions, they make for an easy way to store your line quickly on the stream, whether the rod is collapsed or partially extended. When not in use, the keepers retract and store against the rod, out of the way with nothing extra to carry. You can secure the hook behind a rubber band or hair elastic, though some anglers will simply embed the hook in the cork grip, something I cannot bring myself to do. I usually leave the line on these keepers when fishing frequently or when moving from spot to spot, ready to cast in seconds.

### accessories

Fly boxes, of course, come in an endless variety. Almost anything you choose to store your flies in will work. As we will see later, the traditional tenkara fisherman carries a limited number of flies, sometimes based on tradition but always limited by simplicity. We are going to discuss flies a little later. For now, remember that even fly choice is influenced by tenkara's philosophy of simplicity: Don't overdo it.

To my mind, the weight of the box is the most important consideration. Simple foam fly boxes closed by small magnets have much in their favor. The fact that they float is another advantage, especially in swift water. I have found the magnets handy to temporarily hold a fly, too. Some boxes are better at protecting the hackles of dry flies—an important consideration. Boxes that have removable fly-threaders or nippers with threaders built in can be a great aid to those whose vision or dexterity makes tying on a fly tedious, and are more reliable than any other threading aid. They are quite expensive, however; most sewing needle threaders work fine and at a fraction of the cost.

Dry-fly floatant is rarely if ever needed in tenkara fishing. Dry-fly gels and aerosol sprays seem a needless complication when you are fishing the short drifts and shallow subsurface that characterize tenkara. Blotting your dry fly on your shirt or kerchief or a brisk back-and-forth false cast

will dry your fly quite reasonably. Should we be introducing silicone and hydrocarbon mixes to our streams, no matter how small the amount?

A hemostat (more properly, a needle holder and not a forceps), especially with built-in scissors, is a convenient addition, the smaller the better as long as it fits your fingers. Sometimes there is no more effective way to remove a hook, and the cutting edge is generally all you need for line preparation, though some will insist on nippers (similar to a nail clipper and giving a finer cut). I like hemostats in black or with a quick spray of muting paint. Shiny metal will spook fish. I use the hemostat to tie knots quickly and with much more dexterity than I can manage with cold hands. (I'll show you how to tie quickly with the hemostat in a later chapter.) I clip mine to my shirt pocket flap for easy access and have yet to lose one. Some people attach them to a zinger, a spring-loaded safety cord that can be pinned to a shirt or vest, but these seem to always end up wrapped around something. Nippers do better on a zinger than hemostats.

And speaking of vests, some anglers love the convenience and the multiple pockets of the fishing vest, as well as the traditional look. If you like them, search for vests that have simple and secure closures, with few line-snagging tags and very little exposed Velcro. They should also be lightweight and comfortable, especially around the shoulder and neck. "Shorties" enable you to wade into deeper water without soaking.

Rather than a vest, I prefer a small fanny pack, which easily holds all I need for a day on the stream, including lunch, a raincoat, and a water bottle. I twist it in front of me to access its contents. It has several small pockets to keep me organized, and a neck yoke to hold it higher and convert it to a chest pack for deep water. On shorter fishes when my truck will be near, I leave the pack behind; all I need fits in my shirt pocket. When I teach, I use a small chest pack that keeps tippet, magnifying glasses, and replacement flies handy. This is my preferred pack for canoe and kayak fishing too.

Shoulder bags are comfortable and have a traditional look, doubling as a creel if needed. They have a tendency to bang around a bit when hiking rough terrain, however, and can swing in front of you when bending over to land a fish. Bags with a belt or waist clip are better. Neck lanyards are rightly popular too, though an alligator clip to your shirt is needed to prevent similar swinging. They certainly keep everything handy, although having such a clatter of gear and tippet at the ready is not as pressing with tenkara.

A fish net can be a help in landing a fish, extending your reach and gaining control of a flopping fish more quickly than bringing one to hand. Soft rubber netting is easier on fish, and certainly heavily knotted cord nets are rough, and tend to snag fishing line and hooks. Japanese anglers favor a round net called a *tamo* with a short handle while Catskill anglers like a teardrop shape and slightly longer handle. Traditionally, Japanese include a bit of deer antler in their net design, thought to protect the angler on the stream. In the backcountry, nets tend to get snagged on brush easily. Capturing the net, with a rubber band on the handle, is a trick Gary Borger (the great fly-fishing instructor) passed on to me, and helps in avoiding snags, yet releases quickly. In the thickest of backcountry, nets are extraneous in my view, and many anglers dispense with them completely. From a boat or canoe though, nets are nearly essential. Proper handling is necessary with either method to ensure fish survival, such as wetting the hands before handling.

Adding bug juice, sunscreen, a lighter or waterproof matches, and an LED headlamp are sensible precautions. An emergency campfire in the backcountry has provided welcome warmth more than once, and a headlamp sure makes it easier to hike out in the dark. I also like to protect my hands from sun exposure with lightweight, fingerless gloves. (Skin cancers are most common on the back of hands, as well as forehead, top of the ears, and the neck area of the upper chest.) Polarized sunglasses and a hat with a dark, light-absorbing brim on the underside are a must, both to see fish and to protect eyes and face from sun and wayward hooks. Polarized lenses should have wide coverage and a way to get them out of the way when you need close-up vision; neck straps are fine as are clip-ons.

Accidental skin hooking does happen, and is much easier to remedy if everyone in your party uses barbless hooks. As a lakeside physician for many years, I've used the following trick hundreds of times and it is almost always successful, even with a buried barb. First, with fishing line or a shoestring, make a loop around the hook bend. Then as you push down firmly on the eye of the hook, give the loop of line an abrupt firm tug. The hook comes out almost pain free. But be careful . . . it can go flying.

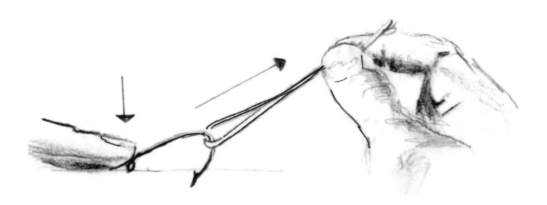

Wading in the summer requires only an old pair of tennis shoes for foot protection. Dedicated wading shoes that drain and grip are better. Sandals, without toe protection, will sooner or later result in a laceration. Hip waders are perhaps the best all-around protection for small streams. Felt soles offer a slightly better grip, but rubber soles are much better for the walk in and they don't ice up during late season fishing. Waist high or chest waders offer the most complete protection, and, especially in breathable fabrics, remain comfortable in the summer heat. Kneeling and squatting is drier in bibs too. All waders will leak eventually it seems, especially if you do much crawling. Knee protectors help, and shin pads additionally ease water pressure when wading fast water. Try the ones made for paintball; they even come in camouflage. One last option, which is great for backpackers, is the river overshoe, which pulls on over your hiking boots and makes very effective hippers. You leave your boots on so you don't have to cache them somewhere streamside.

Invasive species such as didymo, zebra mussels, and mud snails and whirling disease are serious and growing problems for our waters and native fish. The trend away from felt soles, which can transport invasive algae and larva, toward rubber cleats is not a substitute for thoroughly cleaning and drying your gear. The most important step is to clean any mud or algae off your gear at streamside, with a brush if need be. Cleaning at home with diluted chlorine, full-strength vinegar, very hot or salty water, or simply allowing gear to dry five days will further prevent these dangerous hitchhikers. If you do use these solutions, rinse thoroughly to prevent gear damage.

Finally, you may want to consider a wading staff. I use the same carbon trekking pole I use for hiking, which has saved me from many a spill. Old ski poles are a cheap alternative. Consider a rubber tip or duct tape padding if your aluminum staff is a bit noisy. A simple wooden staff works too, but I don't like to rely on streamside limbs, except in a pinch. Attaching a length of line between the handle of your staff and your belt allows you to drop the pole without worry, if you need your other hand to land a fish, for instance. With tenkara fishing, you can easily fish with one hand while steadying yourself with the other, unlike traditional fly fishing that requires two-handed line handling. Walking while casting is *not* a good idea though . . . both will suffer.

Cold weather fishing requires a few extras, including a change of clothes in a dry bag, gloves, and a pocket heat pack, which is admittedly a luxury. (Drop a heat pack into your waders for a quick warmup.) Winter fishing requires an obligatory thermos of coffee or tea, which does a better job of warming one than a flask of spirits. Of course the most important cold weather gear is the clothing you wear. Layers are important, as sweating can be as much a danger as getting wet. I think fleece is grand, but I won't argue against your rag wool either. And for heaven's sake wear a warm toboggan hat and give up your baseball cap in winter. A modern wool-blend sock, perhaps with a thin liner, is best for keeping your feet warm, which may be the first body part to get cold. Synthetic socks retain dampness inside waders.

There are many other gadgets that may add to your knowledge or enjoyment. A seine or fish-tank net (for sampling aquatic insects—a cheesecloth sack over your fish net works nicely too), magnifying loop, binoculars (I carry a 0.8-ounce monocular), and a stream thermometer can be interesting and fun additions. But remember, the more gear you take the more weighted down you will be and the more you can lose or break. More importantly, though, the more gear you take the more you will be tempted to fiddle rather than fish. I especially admire the angler whose kit is simple but whose approach to the water is elegant.

---

## Sources from Pages 9-23

1. Hanneman, William, www.common-cents.info.
2. Likely a shortening of "lily yarn," referring to the manufacturing method, patented in 1923 in Kyoto. Prior to this it was referred to as *hebikuchi,* or "snake mouth," for its resemblance to the tongue of a snake.
3. The common convention of calling nylon line "monofilament" and fluorocarbon line "fluorocarbon" is used here, though both are single filaments of synthetic fiber.

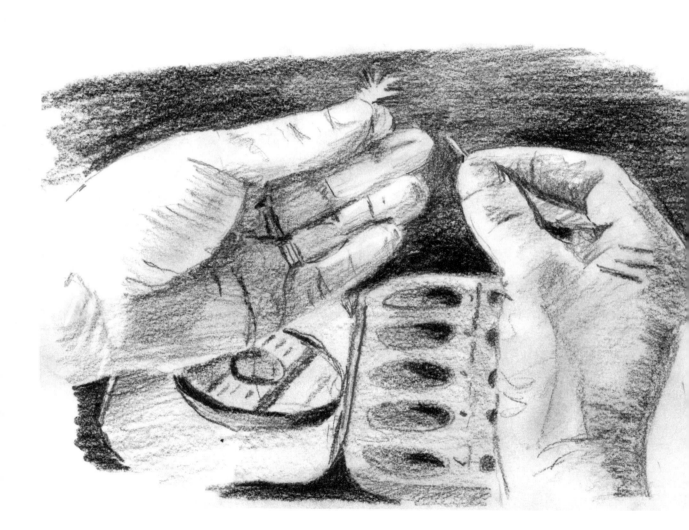

# rigging easily

AS NO MAN IS BORN AN ARTIST, NO MAN IS BORN AN ANGLER.

—Izaak Walton

**Setting up the tenkara rod is easy.** After extending the rod, you will only need one or two knots: the first to occasionally tie on a new tippet, and the second to tie on your fly. The simplest approach is to add tippet with a loop-to-loop junction and to tie on the fly with whatever knot your father taught you.

In the following pages you'll find several different knots that do the same thing. It is an understatement to say anglers have their knot preferences and prejudices. But there is no test ever devised that proves the worthiness of a knot so much as a wildly jumping rainbow trout. As you fish, you will discover your personal preferences. My advice is to pick a few knots and practice them so that you can tie them consistently and with cold hands in fading light.

## rod to line

The furled line is attached to the rod tip with a simple larkshead or girth hitch. Tie an overhand knot in the small line attached to the tenkara rod tip, the lilian. This serves as a simple stop to the hitch. Now bend the loop of the furled line back on itself, as illustrated. Guide the lilian through the hitch and pull the hitch tight.

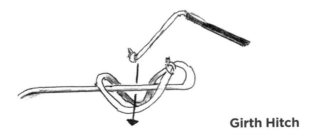

**Girth Hitch**

There are several ways to attach level lines. My preference is to tie a simple overhand knot around the standing part of the line to form a loop. I feed the lilian through the loop twice and tighten. To loosen the knot at the end of the day, I simply pull on the tag end with my hemostats; if you put a stopper knot (figure eight or overhand) on the tag, you can simply loosen it by hand. How easy is that?

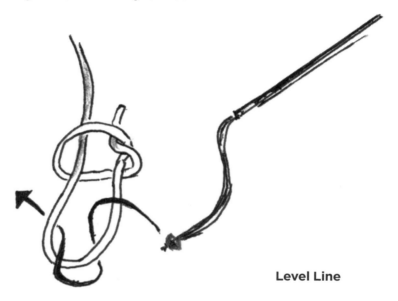

**Level Line**

Another way to rig level lines is to simply convert it with a loop made from line backing. Then you can attach the line with the girth hitch just like you do with the furled line. Attach a loop of Dacron backing (made with a simple overhand loop with the backing doubled) to the mono. (A perfection loop in the mono works.) Leave a quarter inch tag on the backing to make unrigging easy. This is even faster when changing lines frequently.

### line to tippet

Tippet is the final section to which the fly is attached. Since the furled line comes with a loop, adding the tippet to the line with a loop is very easy. Pass a loop of tippet over the loop of the furled line, then feed the tail of the tippet through the same loop. This is called a loop-to-loop connection.

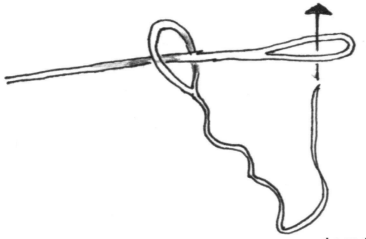

**Loop-to-Loop**

There are a number of ways to tie the loop in the end of your tip-pet. A simple double surgeon's loop will work. The loop is formed with a doubled-up tippet and a two-turn overhand knot.

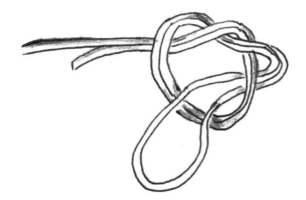

**Double Surgeon**

A double figure-eight loop is another easy method that takes little time to tie. It is simply a figure-eight knot tied with a doubled-up tippet to make a loop.

**Figure-Eight**

My preference though is a perfection loop since it is "in-line," and with a little practice can be tied quickly. Make a loop by crossing behind the standing line, so the tag is pointing right. Now go around again, making a second loop in front and pinching the tag *behind* the first loop. You can use your middle finger to pinch it against the back of the index finger or just add it to the index and thumb pinch. Now take the remaining tag around front and split the two loops, laying it down in the pinch of your finger and thumb. Simply reach through the first loop and grab the second loop (capturing the tag in between the two loops) and pull tightly.

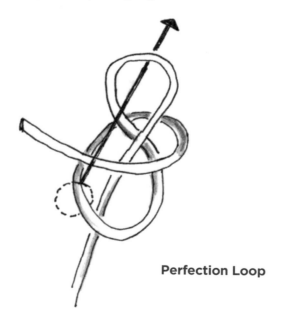

**Perfection Loop**

Loop-to-loop connections are just fine, but there is a new gadget, called a tippet ring, that can make tying lines even easier, and also protect them from wear. Some furled lines come with a tippet ring attached already. Just tie to the ring exactly like you would tie to a hook. I like a uni knot for this task. If your furled line does not have a tippet ring, one can be added easily with a small length of monofilament.

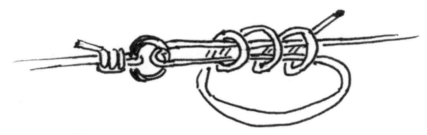

**Uni Knot to Tippet Ring Connection**

An alternative way of attaching tippet to a level line is to tie a stopper knot in the line and tighten a loop on it as illustrated. Tenkara master Dr. Hisao Ishigaki uses this method to tie on his tippet.

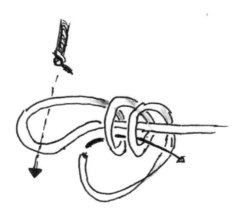

**Ishigaki Tippet Connection**

Lastly, the traditional double surgeon's knot can be used to attach tippet. It is simply an overhand knot doubled. The only drawback to this simple approach is that you lose a bit of your level line every time you tie on tippet.

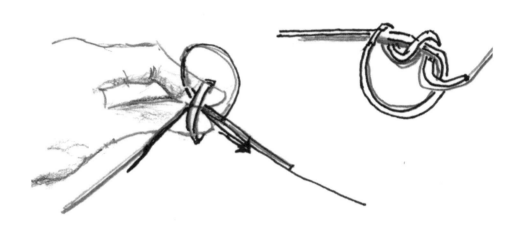

**Double Surgeon Tippet Connection**

A quick way to tie this is to pinch the two pieces of fluorocarbon, then wrap your finger and thumb twice. Pass the ends back over the windings and then through.

### tippet to fly

To attach your fly to the tippet, many anglers prefer a Davy knot, which is simply an overhand knot with the tag tucked. This knot, popularized by fly fisher Davy Wotten, requires a trick however, if it is to have any strength at all. This knot *must* be started with the tippet passing from beneath in a down-turned eyehook and tightened by tugging the standing end, not the tag. Another trick is to hold the tag in your teeth next to the fly when tightening, wetting it while pulling the standing end. This serves to moisten the knot and prevent friction as you tighten the knot. If the tag in your teeth is small enough, it usually doesn't even need to be trimmed. Super fast, this knot is the best knot to preserve tippet and the fastest fly changer of all time, and thus popular with many competition anglers.

**Davy Knot**

Other knots like the clinch, Harvey, and Orvis can be used to tie on flies and are perfectly fine. The Harvey, for instance, guarantees that the fly comes off the tippet in a straight line. Ishimura uses the uni knot. I use the Davy except for bigger flies, then I use the Eugene Bend.

To tie a Eugene Bend with a hemostat, after threading the fly, form a simple loop in the tag. While pinching the loop over the standing line, reach through the loop with the hemostat tip to one side of the standing line and wind the loop around the standing line three times. Now grab the tag and pull it through and tighten. Popularized by Bruce Harang, this quick knot is easy even when tying with cold hands. When the knot is correctly cinched to the eye, you will feel a reassuring "click."

**Quick Eugene Bend**

For extra credit, you can "snell" the dry fly using this knot, too. Instead of tying that uni with the fly above the loop as above, let the fly drop down the standing part of the tippet. Now tie the same knot, but before tightening on the now empty loop, take the whole fly and pass it partway through the formed loop, tightening the knot on the shaft of the fly behind the eye.

### droppers

In most circumstances, fishing with more than one fly increases your odds. Tie on a dropper and double your chances.

The standard way is to simply tie a length of tippet to the hook bend with a uni or clinch knot. This is fine if you are fishing a hopper-dropper or dry-dropper combination. But with the hook of the first fly bound and under tension, it lowers the effectiveness of the upper fly.

For two or more subsurface flies you have a couple choices. One is to simply tie a perfection loop in a piece of tippet and saddle-loop it over the standing line above the existing tippet knot. I can put this on and take it off at will. This is a good way to add a leg for bead or shot weight too. Keep it short though or you'll start tangling.

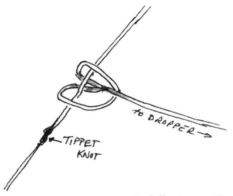

**Saddle Loop Dropper**

An alternative is to just make a big tippet loop (it should be half the distance you would like between the dropper fly and the anchor fly). Take the tag of the loop back to the point where you want the first dropper. Tie in a triple surgeon's knot right there, and cut one leg of the formed loop a little longer than you want the dropper to be. Then just tie on the flies to the two legs formed when you cut the loop. The short leg is your dropper and the long your anchor or point fly.

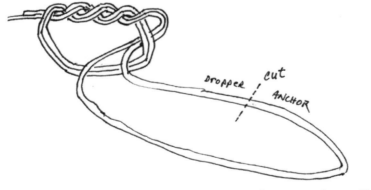

**Surgeons Loop Dropper**

Of course you can just leave your tag long when you tie your tippet on the tippet ring and use that as a leg too. But I often add a dropper after I've given a single fly a workout, since casting with a single fly is more accurate and, I think, more fun.

### knot advice

These knots are more than you'll ever need to fish tenkara. Don't be intimidated. Spending thirty minutes at home with some spare monofilament is all it takes to commit them to memory. When you first start fishing, on-stream knots and changing flies can be a little frustrating, especially when you want to hurry up and fish. Here are a few things that help.

You might like clip-on (to glasses or hat) magnifiers, which help old eyes enormously. I am practically helpless without them. When you thread a fly or form a knot, do so against an uncluttered background (pants leg for instance). Threaders are the most reliable way to get the tippet through the eye of the hook. Some nippers have a threader built in and one even has a magnifier, though I don't prefer them to a separate threader. Sewing needle threaders do work for thin tippet and are the most compact solution. The anvil-shaped magnetic threaders work fairly well too, but there is a trick: Place the fly so the bend is facing up the gutter. After feeding the cleanly cut tippet, pinch it against the threader. Then you can lift the fly to test for successful threading without dropping it. Remember, wet your knot before tightening and always test your knot with a firm tug before risking that next cast on an untested knot.

Though rigging a tenkara rod is very simple, take time to mindfully prepare for the stream. The first cast or two sometimes sets a pattern for the day, so slow down and be aware of where that long rod tip is wiggling.

After you are rigged up, take at least a moment or two to watch the water for signs of fish, then plan your approach. Because many of the streams I fish are tight with brush, my first cast of the day will often be a bow and arrow cast. (You'll see why in the chapter on casting.) By easing into the stream you increase your chances of a more productive and relaxing day of fishing. And after all, isn't that why you came?

# CHAPTER 4
## dance of the dry fly

MOST MEN FISH THEIR WHOLE LIVES WITHOUT KNOWING THAT IT IS
NOT FISH THEY ARE AFTER.

—Henry David Thoreau

Tenkara means "from the heavens" in Japanese, and perhaps refers to
the gentle, almost breeze-soft presentation of the fly. Dry-fly fishing is
thus an ideal technique to showcase tenkara's strengths and introduce
the beginner to fly fishing in general.

Dry flies, of course, are the delicate flies that are made to resemble
insects floating on the surface of water. They are usually made with small
bristly feathers wound tightly around a hook shaft. The feathers' tips,
called hackles, allow the fly to float softly while dimpling the surface.
Fishing with dry flies is the most visual of approaches since all the action
takes place on the water surface.

A very good first step to understanding dry-fly fishing would be to simply observe insects from a comfortable position on your favorite stream,
especially in the cool of the day when they're more active. A pair of compact
binoculars will help. The flitting, diving, incautious aerobatics of flying insects
indicates frenzied mating and egg laying. Check the bushes and grasses at
the stream edge for insects maturing and drying their wings. Watch closely
for any insects that land on the water; you may see exactly what is being
eaten and how it is gobbled. Gather an impression of the color and size of
these insects as they interact with the surface of the stream. Most of all sense
their quiet; you must strive to be just as quiet.

The surface of the water is where birth as well as death takes place
for most aquatic insects. The surface is a barrier for the immature insect
forms, called nymphs, which live in the gravel and silt on the bottom,
and nothing illustrates this better than the lifecycle of the mayfly. As the

nymph prepares to become an adult flying form, it fills with a highly light-refractive bubble, and floats and swims toward the surface. It struggles to break through the surface tension and emerge from its shuck, and dries itself enough to become airborne, hopefully without attracting notice by predator fish. Dry flies that sit low in the water in the head-up position represent these emergers.

At the other end of this brief lifecycle, the adult female, after mating in-flight, returns to the surface to lay her eggs. The mating dance of the male typically consists of an up and down gyration from which this stage gets its name, spinner. So single-minded is this reproductive urge that the adult cannot eat, and has replaced its digestive organs with reproductive organs. Exhausted, the female collapses with outstretched wings and depleted body. She becomes an easy meal for the trout, though not nearly as nutritious as the juicy nymph.

Most of the dry flies you use can be easily tied at home, adding more fun to your sport. As you begin fishing tenkara, choose a standard dry fly such as a Parachute Adams. As a "general" fly, it can represent a variety of insect silhouettes. After observing the insect life near the surface of a stream, you might choose something more specific. Never forget what you are trying to imitate.

Start with a #14 hook. If you are used to lure fishing, you are going to be a little shy about using something so small, but the biggest payoff of fly fishing in general and tenkara in particular is the ability to present these small flies without a splashy disturbance, which can spook the fish.

You must plan your approach with care. First, decide where the fish are likely to be holding. Second, patiently and with stealth, place yourself in the best position for the cast. Lastly, while remaining focused, execute your cast and fly presentation.

Let's look at each of these steps in more detail.

## locate the fish

Spotting fish is easy if you can see their "rises," the dimples or splashes as they feed. If they're not feeding on the surface, they will be holding underwater. In this case, reading the currents will provide the main clues to finding them. Fish generally will be located where there is a good mix of food and cover. They need to obtain food with a minimum expenditure of energy, thus they will hold at the edges of stream flow where the water carries insects to their waiting mouths. A line of surface foam or bubbles often marks these feeding lanes. Fish will be near these edges, but prefer to hold in the slack water deflected around rocks, logs, and ledges, places where they don't have to swim hard while they wait. Fish also need nearby cover to which they can retreat if threatened. When there is a combination of a ready supply of incoming food and good protection from current and predators, these spots are called "prime lies."

Prime lies may be obvious, like the cushion of water in front of or behind a boulder or just out of the current behind a fallen log, but they may also be depressions on the stream bottom, which may give no visible clues on the surface. Polarized sunglasses can often reveal underwater hiding places. Analyzing the current deflections, projecting the slope of banks into the bottom topography, and reconnoitering the shadows of lurking fish from a high vantage point are all ways of stalking fish. In nature one should always think in terms of "edges." However, sometimes the only way to test water is to fish it.

## plan your approach

Before you make your first cast, pick the spots from which you can reach your target with a cast. There is generally a best placement if you think it out. It is generally easier to approach from downstream, as fish by their nature will face into the current. There are times though when approaching from upstream makes sense, for instance when overhanging brush make an upstream cast unlikely. Try to select a spot that is at least partially camouflaged and in shadow. Can you utilize boulders and brush to break up your silhouette? Keep your profile as low to the water as you can, kneeling if necessary. Keep the sun at your back if possible, effectively blinding the fish. Be careful your shadow does not fall over

the fish though. Approach with slow patient steps like the stalking heron; sudden moves are the sign of an unfocused angler.

It is wise to plan not just the first cast but how you will move upstream through each section of stream or beat, casting to each likely spot. Can you deliver the cast from the bank or must you risk disturbing the water with a gentle wade? Plan to reduce wading if possible; fish can sense vibration in the water. If you must wade, do so slowly. Any wavelets you can see on the surface can be felt below. Plan your route so that you cast to each likely spot at least three times without spoiling the next. Minimize movement and cast to several lies from the same spot.

Plan how you will deliver the cast. Is there enough room? What kind of cast will be best? Plan to cast above the fish or a suspected lie so as to present a settled fly. How far above depends on the speed of the current, the depth, and visibility in the water. Where is a fish likely to bolt when hooked? Where is the best place to attempt to land him?

## cast with precision

After arriving at your casting spot, again visualize the entire path of your cast from beginning to landing. Nothing is worse than focusing so intently on the target that you aren't aware of the tree branch behind you. Plan your backcast too.

Choose your target, ahead of and to the side of your suspected fish. Focus on the one piece of water, no bigger than a floating paper plate, where you want the fly to land. Consider starting your cast with a smooth exhalation, just like a marksman pulling the trigger. The first cast to a spot is always the most likely to stimulate a bite; make it a good one. It is much better to hoard your casts, fishing few but more precise casts, than to cast repeatedly. Be ready; fish most often take a fly soon after it lands.

Nearby current that is faster than the water in which the fly is drifting can ruin your presentation. Try not to let the current grab your line and tug the slower-moving fly. A dragging fly with a wake does not resemble an insect. A high reach and a light touch that leaves neither too much line on the water nor takes up all the slack will help avoid drag. Tenkara rods, with their long reach, enable you to keep everything but the tippet off the water. More than the western "high sticking," tenkara actually allows much longer line lift. (For instance, assuming a conservative right angle between rod and line, a thirteen-foot tenkara rod could keep eighteen feet of line off the water compared to twelve for a nine-foot rod. The contrast is made even greater when considering line weight sag and the strain of holding an extended western rod and reel for long hours.)

Try to keep any line on the surface in water moving the same speed as the fly. This means casting upstream or slightly across stream and keeping your tip elevated as you follow the fly. As the fly drifts downstream, adjust the amount of slack by raising and lowering the rod tip.

If your focus is good, you will constantly observe the water around the fly as you keep it in your field of vision. You may see the flashing silver of an interested fish nearby, or the white of his mouth with a take. Sometimes a fish shows interest by breaking the surface behind your cast, as if to ask, "What was that?" Show him again.

As a fish takes your fly, you will often be surprised at the vigor with which it breaks your reverie, launching from below and splashing explosively. At other times, it may be a sipping take, mere lips breaking the surface then running deep with its meal. Either way, you must be ready to lift your rod like a flag with a crisp snap of the wrist, capturing your quarry and rewarding your stream craft, stealth, and focus.

The dry-fly cast encompasses the essentials of tenkara fly fishing, though I must confess that tenkara wet fly or subsurface fishing is, in fact, more traditional and perhaps more productive. (We will explore subsurface fishing soon.) In fact, certain dry flies can be fished wet as they become soaked, with great effectiveness.

Remember to execute mindfully. Athletes may recognize this as "being in the zone." Your prize will not only be plenty of exciting fishing but the disciplining of the mind as well. The distractions of the world and the ego will often evaporate, leaving room for clarity and confidence and, most of all, great fun.

In Japan there is a much-prized aesthetic called *wabi sabi. Wabi* implies, first and foremost, a simplicity through which a person obtains a degree of harmony, balance, and understanding of their place in the world. Its meaning is rooted in a sense of spareness, almost poverty, in which one finds contentment in the most basic of possessions, an acceptance of imperfection. Through this simplicity one is able to experience a sense of peace and, most of all, authenticity. *Sabi* is the character of natural materials that show signs of the aging process and the mark of time. It reminds us of the impermanence of all things. When tenkara is approached with simplicity, mindfulness, patience, and an appreciation for the natural environment and our place within it, it is certainly wabi sabi.

When, after a patient stalk, your dry fly softly lands within inches of the placement you visualized, drifting without drag across the cool shadow of a prime lie, then you have already landed the prey you seek.

# CHAPTER 5

# underwater rooms

THE COMMON EYE SEES ONLY THE OUTSIDE OF THINGS, AND JUDGES
BY THAT, BUT THE SEEING EYE PIERCES THROUGH AND READS THE
HEART AND THE SOUL.

—Mark Twain

**Have you ever navigated across a room in the dark,** knowing where the furniture was without seeing it, and then finding the light switch? Subsurface fishing is similar. When you are fishing wet flies well, you are visualizing the fly as it drifts and swings underwater without seeing it or the fish. You anticipate where the best lies are as you guide the fly through these likely spots based on your reading of the surface currents, signs of underwater obstructions, the topography of bank and shade, and your intuitive feeling for the water. The best wet fly anglers develop a sixth sense about the fly's location and appearance, and can often anticipate the take with consistent accuracy.

Subsurface fishing is ideal for the tenkara rod. Because of its long reach, the tenkara rod can stay in touch with the tiny movements of the fly all through its drift. Tenkara rods allow the angler to keep most of the line off the water, while leading the subsurface fly through the best lies. Because the majority of the time trout feed below the surface, subsurface fishing is usually the most productive type of fishing, day in and day out.

There are three basic types of flies used for subsurface fishing: the nymph, the Soft-Hackle wet fly, and the streamer. The nymph is a slightly tapered or cone-shaped fly, with thorax or chest larger than abdomen, some indication of legs, and generally weighted. The wet fly has a sparser body and uses undulating feather hackles to represent the actively swimming emerger. The streamer is a larger, streamlined fly, whose waving feathers or moving fur represents a fleeing fish such as a minnow or fry.

**Nymph**          **Soft Hackle Wet**          **Streamer**

## nymphs

Tenkara allows for excellent control when drifting a nymph with the current. By casting upstream and keeping your rod tip nearly even with the nymph, tip held high, you should allow a small amount of tippet slack to be the lead for your nymph. Much like the leash on a dog, you want to keep track of things without losing control, yet allowing some slack, while tightening up from time to time. Keep your eye on this slack at the point where the line enters the water, as the nymph bounces and skips across the bottom. Watch the line for anything out of the ordinary, as takes near the bottom can be very subtle. With this cast you are nicely imitating an immature insect that has lost its grip on the bottom gravel and is tumbling into danger. Try hard to visualize this tumble in three dimensions. Add a lift of the rod tip, tightening the line, and you are imitating a nymph seeking the surface.

Fish feeding on nymphs typically lie in the bottom twelve inches of the stream. When fishing nymphs, be sure to use enough weight to get to the bottom. The faster the water, the more weight will be needed. Ideally the nymph itself had enough weight built into it when it was tied. This makes for an easier cast and lighter feel, a real consideration with a soft tenkara rod. I like bead-headed nymphs for this reason.

However, you can add split shot to a tag or on the tippet above a nymph. Putting the weight on a tag rather than putting weight above the fly on the tippet allows for slightly more sensitivity in the line, allow-ing you to more readily detect a bite. Shot on the tag will break off if snagged on the bottom, thus saving the fly. Glass, brass, and tungsten beads held on the tag with a jammed toothpick work well too. Placement of the weight no more than fifteen inches above the nymph helps ensure the nymph will stay near the productive bottom. Always use nontoxic shot; lead weight can kill waterfowl.[1]

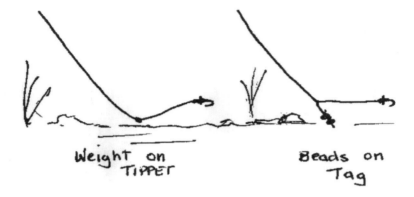

Weight on TIPPET    Beads on Tag

When fishing nymphs, make sure to cast far enough upstream to allow the nymph enough time to sink to the bottom before drifting into the target zone. This is especially important with a tenkara rod, where you will have a somewhat limited reach. When casting heavily weighted nymphs, slow your upstream cast to avoid tangling your line; lob the weighted flies upstream. There is a fine line between too little and too much weight. Adjust the amount frequently if you are having little success. A few inches deeper can make a difference when fish are sluggish.

Remember as well that the heavier your tippet the slower your sink rate. Each transition to a thinner-diameter tippet lowers drag by 35 to 40 percent. With a heavier tippet it is more difficult to get to that target twelve inches. Fluorocarbon density also aids sink rate.

The tenkara traditionalist will eschew added weight, and indeed it does change the feel of the cast and drift. In moderate water, casting technique can compensate for less weight by casting further upstream. This allows a deeper penetration by the unweighted fly.

### soft-hackle wet flies

The Soft-Hackle wet fly wiggles through the water. The hackle is called "soft" given that it is usually made from hen or partridge feathers, more pliable than the stiffer hackles used in dry flies. Soft-Hackles are tied so that water pressure "works" them, alternately collapsing and expanding the feather collar. The wet fly is the most traditional of British chalkstream flies, but the Japanese have a traditional wet fly, too.

Japanese flies, or kebari, are generally so simple and versatile yet effective that they are the exclusive fly of some anglers. Different regions of Japan claim different styles of this fly, but they all have simplicity in common, both in construction and in fishing technique. Kebari flies are most often fished in the top six inches of water, and are cast somewhat harder to break the surface tension, then retrieved in pulses. If cast further upstream and allowed to sink, the kebari fly can be used to explore greater depths. Cast dry, it can be worked on the surface. With its variety of presentations, the kebari is a very versatile fly. Traditional tenkara flies have reverse hackles with the tips pointing forward toward the hook eye, increasing water resistance and providing for greater animation. The texture of the hackles can be used to alter the movement.

Wet flies use motion to attract fish, which allows them to be fished from the top to the bottom of the water column. Given that there is less concern for drag, they can be fished both across a stream and downstream. Fishing two or three wet flies on the same tippet is a traditional western means of increasing your odds. This lineup of flies gave the original meaning to a "cast of flies."

The wet fly is usually cast across a stream and allowed to swing downstream. Lifting and dropping the tip of your rod causes the wet fly to follow. These gentle lifts can be done anytime during the cast but are very effective when approaching a suspected lie. Remember that a sluggish fish is like a sports fan in a recliner . . . he's not going to move far to eat.

Though wet flies seem out of favor with western anglers, their adaptability, if not their venerable history, should keep some wet flies in your box. Besides, they work! The sensitive tip of the tenkara rod allows working these flies quite nicely. I predict that with the growth of tenkara, we will see a resurgence of the Soft-Hackle wet fly. The wet fly fisherman always stays alert with a "tight line" leading to the underwater rooms his fly is exploring.

### streamers

Streamers are wet flies that resemble feeder fish, both in profile and motion. They are cast across a stream. Because feeder fish are the preferred food of larger fish, streamers are the first choice when prospecting for bigger fish. Streamers can be given a darting motion very effectively with the tenkara rod. Observing minnows in a shallow spot is a good way to picture the motion you are trying to create. Fish a streamer broadside to or slightly away from a suspected lie. (No frightened baitfish will swim toward a predator fish.) Streamers can be drifted, tumbled, twitched . . . just about any presentation you can imagine. I like a lighter dressing when fishing streamers with tenkara as they cast more gently. Just because the reach of a tenkara rod precludes the traditional stripping of line does not mean that streamers cannot be deadly efficient tenkara flies.

## indicators

All of these subsurface flies can be fished with an indicator, too. In fact, indicators are a big help in faster water and for beginning nymph anglers, though you may find as you improve your fishing skills an indicator becomes optional. I use them regularly if the water is tumbling or riffled, as they help me see bites on a bouncing line and do not spook fish as badly when the surface is broken. An indicator is any float that suspends a subsurface fly at a specific depth or telegraphs its hidden motion (even if not suspending it). Plastic bubbles are a sturdy favorite for "heavy" or turbulent water while "corkies" are the cork or foam version. Both can spook fish in quieter water. Make sure the indicator you use can be moved up and down to easily adjust for depth, and use the smallest one that will work.

Using a buoyant dry fly as an indicator with a subsurface fly tied to the bend of the hook works well in lieu of an indicator. A grasshopper imitation is a common choice for the dry because it is large, floats well, and is easily followed. This combination is called the "hopper-dropper," and can be very productive on warm days, with fish hitting either fly. Smaller dries like a parachute are used in quieter water.

Yarn added to the line will also serve as an indicator. The yarn can be captured in the knot joining the tippet to the line or tied to the tag of this knot, as well as simply forming a slip-loop mid tippet. For a movable method, tie the yarn to the line with another piece of tippet with a clinch knot or uni knot. Yarn tends to soak easily, though, which necessitates the use of floatant.

For tenkara nymph fishing in moderate water, you can use a foam-strip indicator. To make your own, cut a one-and-a-half-inch to two-inch strip of closed cell foam in the color you prefer, about ⅛ to ¼ inch wide. Fold over one end and whip it with thread. When fishing, feed a loop of line through the foam loop as shown. (Hemostats can be inserted through the stretchable foam loop to grab the line.) Loop the line over the bulk of the indicator and tighten. Leave the loop in the notch of the short leg. This makes it easier to move and prevents kinking. With a heavily weighted fly, two strip indicators set a foot apart work well. A strip indicator is very sensitive and casts well while not requiring floatant, and the direction it points gives important information about the drift.

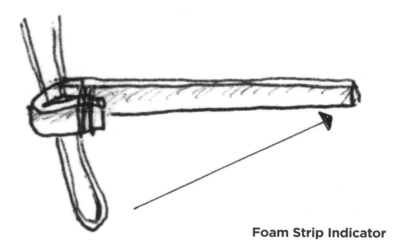

**Foam Strip Indicator**

Tie in a small section of brightly tinted monofilament before the tippet for another easily followed indicator, or better yet two colors in series to give you a sensitive visual display on sly takes. Setting a coil of heavier monofilament in this section (a five-minute boil followed by an overnight freeze with the line wrapped tightly around a bolt will do it) makes it especially visible.

There is evidence that Japanese tenkara anglers may have used floats in the past, and I have found them very useful in helping beginner anglers catch their first fish. The tenkara angler should not feel pressed to do without them. However, most tenkara anglers will jettison them eventually, opting for the increased sensitivity and ease of casting that is found with a light and less "gear-laden" line. The short distance to your fly and ultrasensitive rod tip makes this transition easier than it sounds. Concentration is, however, an essential ingredient.

Immature insects are found underwater all year long, and fish do seem to be less wary while they're feeding underwater. Fish mostly prefer the bottom, and will often feed on a nymph drifting at their level even when they won't cruise to another level to feed. With less light penetration, fly imitation underwater is easier too. A fly that gives just a general impression of food will often be taken where a dry fly would have resulted in refusals.

The best anglers focus on the area of water through which the fly is moving, the line where it touches the water, and the feel transmitted through the sensitive rod tip to the grip. Keep as much line off the water as possible. This is one of the major advantages of tenkara fishing, so practice holding the line away from the surface. Drag remains important underwater, so lead the fly with a bit of slack tippet when dead-drifting a subsurface fly. Any unusual movement in the fly could result in it being refused. As you drift the fly, look for an excuse for a quick, hook-setting motion, especially when you think that fly is drifting through a likely spot. I am surprised how often a subtle bump turns out to be a bite when responded to quickly. Some nymphing instructors say that you should arbitrarily hook-set at least once during the drift. Fish can nibble gently underwater, and we likely miss as many as half or more of the bites. After all, underwater prey can't simply fly away. The shadowed depths give fish the home court advantage.

---

## Sources from Pages 45-51

1. Lead sinkers (not just bird shot) are a major cause of death in loons, cranes, and swans as demonstrated by autopsy studies at Tufts University, Sidor et al. 2003 and Pokras et al. 2008.

# CHAPTER 6

# the simplest cast in fly fishing

IN THE WOODS, TOO, A MAN CASTS OFF HIS YEARS, AS THE SNAKE
HIS SLOUGH, AND AT WHAT PERIOD SOEVER OF LIFE IS ALWAYS A
CHILD.

—Ralph Waldo Emerson

One of the strengths of tenkara lies in its cast. It's so simple that in a short time you will be able to execute it without thinking, allowing you to concentrate on the approach and presentation.

A beginner can use a tenkara rod to place a fishable fly immediately without instruction. (In fact, no instruction is often a better approach if you are introducing a child; just let them fish without critique.) However, a bit of thought about casting and a little practice can make your tenkara experience more fruitful. This chapter will show you how easily you can accomplish this.

A western fly angler will want to compare and modify his or her cast for tenkara. You may never have held such a light and responsive rod before. If you are an experienced angler, expect to overpower a tenkara rod at first. The cast of the tenkara rod is different because of its slower action and its length. As a general rule, all your casting movements will be briefer and less vigorous than with a western fly rod. In contrast to western fly casting, very small wrist and forearm motion is often all that is needed. The abrupt stop or flick at the end of the cast, however, remains important, just as in western casting. Work with the rhythm inherent in the rod. Wait on it. You'll be surprised at how smoothly and efficiently you can cast if you allow the rod to do the work.

### the grip

Since the tenkara rod is so much lighter, the grip is chosen more for accuracy than strength. Placing the index finger along the backbone of the rod or slightly to the side will help develop accuracy and restrain the delicate tenkara cast. It is through the pointed fingertip that tenkara gets much of its precision and uniqueness. As in western fly fishing, you will want to involve your forearm in the motion; however a more relaxed and smaller motion is all that is needed. In fact, the motion of a tenkara cast is often mere inches. With such a lightweight rod, you will be able to cast for a longer time with less fatigue. You will find yourself being able to flick the fly with just a quick hand movement. "Choking up" on the grip or even onto the rod proper can aid accuracy as well as shorten the rod for tight casting. Keep your arm and grip relaxed. Any tension reduces accuracy.

Some tenkara anglers like a "v-grip," which involves moving the index finger off to the side, forming a "v" between thumb and forefinger, with the forefinger pointing down the backbone of the rod. This adds power to the stroke. The placement of the grip can also vary with the direction of a given cast.

### the stance

A balanced stance is helpful in a good cast, but most anglers will do this automatically. When extreme precision is important, tenkara masters often lead slightly with the right foot (for right-handers) helping to aim the rod, thus keeping the trajectory more on line with the arm and the path of the rod. This is called a "closed stance." At its most accurate, the path intersects the fisherman's eyes mid-forehead. With the non-casting arm counterbalancing, hand-on-hip, this tenkara position closely resembles the *en garde* stance of a fencer. When learning, an "open stance" (left foot leading) allows the student to watch his line more easily. Crouching and kneeling are likely positions when fishing too. On the water your stance is more likely determined by the stream. Keep your stance relaxed and yet athletically poised, the stance of a hunter.

## sidearm cast

Remember that the cast primarily does one thing: The flex of the rod pulls the line behind you, then a reversal of this flex pulls it forward again toward the target. The best way to feel this is to simply try a back and forth sidearm motion. You can see how the line forms a loop and then straightens. To better visualize the cast, Misako suggests trying this sidearm casting with yarn attached rather than line. The important thing is to sense this very fundamental back and forth motion. Don't go too fast . . . wait briefly on the backcast to straighten before accelerating forward. This pause is very important. Keep a relaxed grip and work with the rod. Watch as it bends with the load, then releases its energy as the line unrolls. Get a feel for the flow of this motion.

When casting with a tenkara rod, I think it is useful to try to think of moving the tip back and forth around a thinly stretched oval. Go under the oval on the backcast, and over the oval on the forward cast. At the end of the oval, as your rod tip moves toward the target, stop the rod by a brief flick of your pointing index finger. I like to tell students the index finger movement is like scolding the fish. You will see that the line is cast in the direction the tip was moving when you stopped it. This brusque stop of the wrist and arm is what sends the line toward the target. Fly anglers don't cast by pointing the tip directly at the target (like spin anglers) because the tip bends so much. Instead stop the rod while still pointing slightly sideways. I like to compare it to flicking paint on a wall out of a loaded paintbrush. The stop does not have to be hard, but you will find that a full stop with a light squeeze of the grip is best for extended and accurate casts, especially when casting longer lines.

Because the fly is going to end up in the water (we hope), the backcast should be inclined upward by varying degrees. The angle of the backcast is generally higher than with a western rod due to the short line. This is very helpful in avoiding snagging brush. If you do find your fly catching in the flora, angle the backcast up even more.

Gently lift the line from the water and fling it backwards and slightly upwards. After a brief pause in which the line straightens, start the line forward toward your target, stopping your hand once it has the proper momentum, flinging it home. Err on the side of gentleness. Can you feel the smooth application of the rod's bending? Can you see how it does most of the work for you?

Even young anglers can figure a tenkara sidearm cast out within a couple of tries. With practice, the sensation of loading the rod with the weight of the line will soon become second nature, as long as you do not try to force your cast.

Sidearm casting is one of the most useful casts. With its low profile, fish do not easily see it. It fits nicely with an upstream casting plan as you walk along the stream bank, placing most of the cast over the water instead of in the trees. For this reason, if you're a right-handed caster, choose the left bank as you make your way upstream.

I use a sidearm cast frequently to dry a fly that has become soaked, making several vigorous false (back and forth) casts. False casts with tenkara rods are much less likely to whip-crack than with stiffer western rods, so don't be afraid to give it a bit of snap to dry the fly out. False casting over a fish is a sure way to spook it, however. Dry your fly in a different direction.

While the sidearm cast is the one that the tenkara angler will use most often, there are a couple more casts you will find useful.

### overhead cast

Tenkara fishermen in the mountains of Japan traditionally have relied mostly on the overhead cast. This cast is flicked above your shoulder and head and then forward on the same line to the target. It is useful for placing your backcast high above streamside trees. It can also be very accurate.

If you are trained in the "clock face" approach to western fishing, the overhead cast occupies only the wedge from ten o'clock to noon, maybe less. The backcast is composed of a fairly steep and quick pull upward, using the forearm more than the wrist. This resembles the backcast of the western steeple cast. The forward motion is much abbreviated and pulls the line over the top of a very thin oval. Try to keep the line moving along the same trajectory. The loop that is formed as the line goes back and forward is tighter when the cast is on line. A tighter loop is a more accurate loop, and if a loop is narrow it is less likely to catch on things.

However, it is also useful to sometimes break this rule and change the direction of your cast. Although not as efficient, such a cast can help place a fly when there is no clearance immediately behind the target. Also you may want to quickly place your fly off line if you suddenly spot a fish rising.

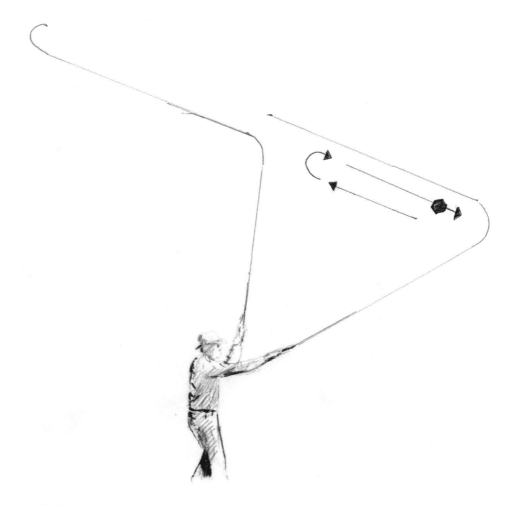

If the rod is directed with a sharp stop, the loop will be tight and less affected by wind. A more arched cast results in a larger loop and a slightly softer cast. The angle varies a bit depending on how far or near from you that you want the fly to land. A more open loop is useful for softer presentations and a brace of more than one fly, just as in western fly casting. Tight loops can throw longer lines and heavier flies.

If the stop is too vigorous, however, you may find the rod tip bouncing back so abruptly that the line piles and shortens the cast. You want this stop to be firm but not jerky. Remember, aim your index finger and squeeze the grip gently; a little bit of abruptness goes a long way. With a short tenkara line, you can tuck a fly into the water nicely with little effort. Use your index finger like an orchestra conductor; there is a delightful rhythm to the tenkara cast.

Tenkara fishing in Japan traditionally uses a wet fly in the fast, broken waters of mountain streams. In this case a fairly hard landing is useful for attracting fish and breaking the surface tension, allowing the fly to sink more easily. In quiet or still water, and especially with dry flies, a softer landing is better. Aiming your fly at a spot a foot above the surface will give you a softer presentation.

## backhand cast

The backhand cast is simply a way to cast on the opposite side of your body. The backhand cast in tenkara fishing is slightly different from its western cousin. It does not need as long a stroke. On the backcast, the

hand is raised toward the opposite shoulder such that the forearm and forehead almost touch, thus casting on the other side of your body. The forward stroke attempts to present a straight line from the backward stroke, using, as always, a flicking index finger.

A backhand cast is very useful when wind is coming from the casting side and you want your fly and its sharp hook to stay safely downwind. It is also necessary when wading upstream on the "wrong side" from your dominant hand. A backhand cast is useful in presenting a fly to some more difficult lies and is a sign of a practiced fisherman. Of course, as an alternative, you may want to learn to cast with both hands, which is surprisingly easy with a tenkara rod.

## roll cast

When an angler has little room behind him for a backcast, a roll cast is often the way to go. Since tenkara lines are relatively short compared to western rods, this cast is almost always executed with a sidearm motion. As the fly is fished back or lifted slowly toward the angler, and while the line still has some contact with the water, simply load the rod with a slight

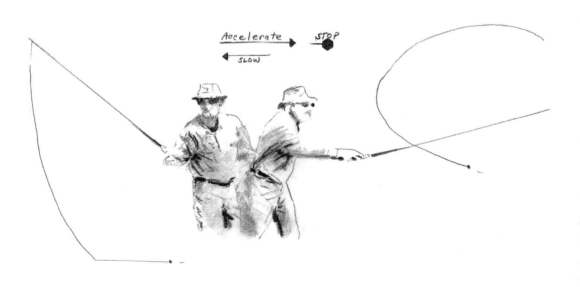

up-and-back pull, using the water to anchor the end of the line and fly, then accelerate toward the target, ending in an abrupt stop, flicking the fly toward its target. The water contact helps to load the rod and should be roughly on the same line as the target.

The tip follows a slight oval or roll, important in order to keep the line from tangling. Remember to aim nearly parallel with the water, not in a karate-chop down motion. With the roll cast you must wait for the line as it unrolls toward the target. Since there is only moderate loading, you will sacrifice distance, unless the casting stop is particularly strong and abrupt.

By the way, a quick and forceful roll cast, sent past a snag, can some-times loosen a snagged hook in the water. Make your forward roll past the snag, as vigorous as you can manage; this maneuver is not as effective as with a western rod.

## lob cast
At the beginning of a lob cast, the current of the water is allowed to pull the fly downstream until there is some tension or drag on the line. The

rod then tugs the fly against the current, flipping the fly in the upstream direction. Because of its low profile, this cast is especially effective in the wind. It's a cast that always takes less effort than you'd first expect, and is done with a very relaxed motion. It is my favorite tenkara cast because I enjoy the way the entire line extends upstream with so little effort. With practice you can cast in either direction.

With heavier flies this cast becomes even more of a lob, as the added weight loads the rod. If you're using droppers or indicators this is the ideal cast to prevent tangles, and is perfect for short-line nymph fishing and Euro nymphing. (More about this later.) Of course, it takes a little more muscle to cast heavier flies.

### bow and arrow cast

Sometimes called a slingshot cast, and known in Japan as *yabiki,* the bow and arrow cast is very useful when the brush is particularly tight. I often use it as the first cast of the day. It's a quick way to just get the fly on the water. The line is gathered in a couple loose loops in the non-casting hand (about eight inches is a good size for the loops) pinching the line between thumb and finger. (For shorter lines, just pinch the tippet above the hook without loops.) The rod tip is pulled back, forcing a strong bend

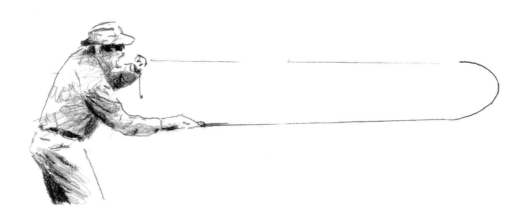

on top of the rod, with the rod tip and tensioned line above the rod shaft. A smooth release will result in a surprisingly effective fly placement. If the hook is hanging below your pinch by no more than eight inches, you won't risk getting snagged. If you are familiar with this cast using western rods, you will be surprised by how much more efficient tenkara rods are.

## underhand cast

For an underhand cast, the oval of the cast's path is in the opposite direction from a more conventional cast. You simply load the rod into the backcast over the top of the oval and let the fly go on the bottom of the oval, like an underhand softball pitch. A variation is the tension-swing cast. Misako, inspired by Bob Clouser's oval casts (in which he maintains rod loading over an oval path), uses this variation for very accurate placement under brush. The tip of the rod, held to the side (anywhere from forty-five degrees to a few feet above the water), is simply pulled backwards in a straight line from the target, allowing the fly line to follow under the rod tip. Stop the rod tip with a brief pause while the line extends behind you.

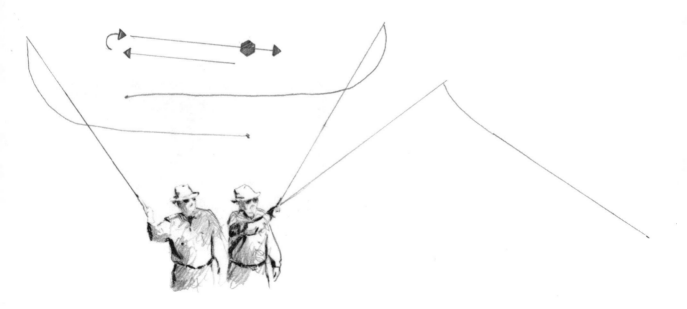

The rod tip then moves on a straight path forward toward the target, pulling the line and fly underhand. The line never goes over the top of the rod. The fly is dropped to the target at the apogee of the forward swing. The line stays below the rod throughout the cast, closer to the water. A little touch is needed to swing the fly in low, and a feel for this cast requires a little practice. With the innovative tension-swing cast, the path of the fly is very narrow, often just a few inches below the rod, and can be used to avoid obstacles that would obstruct other casts.

Acknowledging that the traditional tenkara cast has been fine-tuned over several centuries, it may be wise to emphasize the appearance of a tenkara master casting on the stream. With intense focus and awareness of streamside camouflage, the master places a precise overhead cast into the seam of current or eddy. His backcast is high, thrown over his shoulder and head. His forward cast is accomplished with a brief and precise thrust toward the target. He lands the fly with a bit of firmness that sinks the fly through the surface tension, allowing the fly to sink to the desired depth. By pulsing the tip of his tenkara rod, and as his intuition dictates, he adds lifelike animation to the reverse hackle fly. The drift spent, he tugs the fly against the water tension, sending it over his shoulder for his next cast. Throughout he remains balanced and ready to set the hook.

Tenkara allows for endless variations to the cast, of course. Over time, you will find yourself developing your own casts, unique to your height, strength, fly and rig weight, and home stream characteristics. Though knowing these seven casts might improve your ability to cast in many different situations, the idea is still to simply get a fly to the fish. They don't really care how it gets there. Because all the tenkara variations are so simple, you are allowed to keep your mind on accurate placement, which is, in fact, more important. Intuition will take over if you allow it.

If you are used to casting with a western rod, the adjustments to tenkara really are minor. The casts are basically the same. You will find though that after fishing with a tenkara rod a while, your western fly casting will improve too. Because the tenkara rod must load the rod with the stroke itself, hauling a line is not a method used to overcome casting faults. The next time you cast your western rod, you will notice you are loading it more efficiently. Tenkara makes a great training aid and is a fantastic way to introduce someone to the essentials of fly fishing.

As your casting gets better, and particularly on larger waters, you may want to extend the length of the line you are using for greater reach. Maintaining line tension throughout the entire cast becomes a very important concept when casting a longer line. Italian fly-fishing master Roberto Pragliola describes the efficiency and accuracy of the tight-looped cast, which he calls T.L.T. casting (*Tecnica Lancio Totale,* or Total Casting Technique). At the end of your backcast, your casting arm drifts up a bit. This inscribes the first half of the oval. As the forward cast progresses, the arm extends forward and rotates down a bit before coming to a stop, allowing one to cast the line to full extension. Think of the pattern inscribed made by a drive-rod on a locomotive wheel.

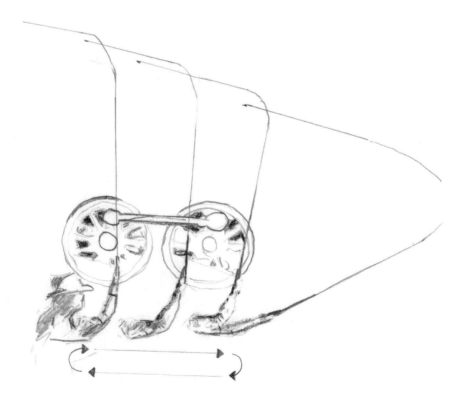

Keeping a bit of tension throughout the cast may bring to mind the Belgium cast, which is essentially a constant-tension cast that starts as a sidearm cast and ends as an overhead cast. The tenkara cast has many of the attributes of this cast, albeit with a smaller oval. Sometimes the oval is so narrow it is hardly recognizable. Other times it is wider and more obvious. For greatest efficiency, the legs of the oval should remain parallel. With increased tension and using a longer fluorocarbon level line, Dr. Ishigaki will cast up to twice the length of the rod, extending the reach of the tenkara rod over thirty feet. Thinking in terms of this oval in your casting is sure to improve your distance and line extension. However, short-range accuracy remains the strength of tenkara.

As you explore the tenkara cast or as you transition from western fly casting to tenkara, keep in mind the basics:

1.  Don't overpower your casts: Tenkara is a restrained, even gentle cast.

2.  Tighter loops mean more control: Tighter loops are formed when the arm movement is brief and brisk, and the backcast and forward cast are on the same line. "Flick that paintbrush."

3.  The fly goes where the tip points: At first, aim the whole length of the rod rather than focusing on the tip; as you become more experienced you will develop "tip awareness."

4.  Lift up your backcasts: By aiming backcasts with at least some elevation, the angler keeps his line from dropping on the water or catching on the grass behind. An elevated backcast also allows for a slight, downward angle on the forward cast. The closer you are to your target, the higher you should elevate your backcast.

5. Stay balanced and relaxed: By remaining lithe in your motions, neither too rigid nor too loose, you will tire less readily and be more accurate in your cast. A stable stance helps. Tension blocks the flow of energy from your feet, through your arms, and all the way to the tip of the rod.

6. Practice accuracy: Aim at a distinct target with every cast. Practice precision. To fish most effectively, accuracy is essential, and is the primary skill that characterizes the accomplished angler.

# CHAPTER 7

# small streams

WE NEED THE TONIC OF WILDNESS, TO WADE SOMETIMES IN MARSHES
WHERE THE BITTERN AND THE MEADOW-HEN LURK, AND HEAR THE
BOOMING OF THE SNIPE; TO SMELL THE WHISPERING SEDGE WHERE
ONLY SOME WILDER AND MORE SOLITARY FOWL BUILDS HER NEST,
AND THE MINK CRAWLS WITH ITS BELLY CLOSE TO THE GROUND.

—Henry David Thoreau

**The small stream is the tenkara specialty.** But it is important to have a thorough understanding of these waters if you want to locate and catch fish. Searching maps and investigating small streams, especially ones passed up by other anglers, can be an adventure in itself.

## small stream quality

The fertility of a stream determines the abundance and size of fish. Chalk streams, also known as limestone streams, are spring-fed streams with water that percolates from limestone beds. They tend to be the most productive. Freestone, granite-bedded, and sandstone streams fed by runoff tend to be the least fertile due to wide swings in water depth, spring flooding, and temperature variations. They are less porous and tend not to favor sustained communities of insects, plants, or fish. Furthermore, in these streams acidification can occur with little chance of neutralization, as opposed to the natural neutralizing effect of limestone. Because spring-fed streams tend to be more fertile both in insect life and aquatic plants, the fish will be bigger and better fed, but also more wary.

Tailwaters, or streams that are supplied and nourished by bottom-release dams, keep water temperatures steady year-round (although their flows can vary widely). Tailwaters are early season favorites as they tend to be warmer, and late summer producers because they stay cooler.

The wide variation in flow though can favor small, rapidly reproducing aquatic insects. Most small streams tend to be a mix of limestone, free-stone, and tailwater, allowing for wide variances in water fertility and fish density, often from place to place on the same stream.

The water quality can be determined partially by examining the clarity of the water and the streambed. Silt and mud runoff covers gravel that is needed for most insect maturation. Silt can kill fish by clogging their gill plates. It blocks sunshine, making bottoms inhospitable to insect life and aquatic plants, and covers fish redds, or nests. Silt can also combine with toxins, prolonging the ill effects of pollutants and oils.

Water temperature determines the level of fish activity. Fish are poiki-lotherms, which means they cannot regulate their own metabolism. Their internal chemistry depends on water temperature, thus their tendency to feed and move is controlled by temperature. Trout feed best in waters that vary from 55 to 65 degrees, and often aren't very active at all until spring temperatures reach 45 degrees. In highly oxygenated water (rif-fled water with waterfalls for example) higher temperatures are tolerated. In alpine regions where these temperatures may never be reached, fish are active at lower temperatures. Species that have arctic origins like the brook trout (really a char) prefer lower temperatures than other "trout." Along the course of a small stream, the temperature can be variable due to tributaries and underground springs and seeps, one of the factors con-tributing to fish density. Deforestation can adversely affect water tem-perature and fish survival. Overheating due to the clearing of streamside vegetation can ruin a stream. Coldwater fish like trout cannot survive high temperatures. When searching for fish in a stream you might want to study the temperature first.

Light penetration can affect fish density too. Bright light on clear, smooth water can send fish to cover like a spotlight on an introvert. Except in the cold days of early spring, when fish may seek warmer shal-lows or huddle up against sunlit rocks, fish will invariably prefer the shad-ows, where they can more easily avoid predators. Light broken by a riffled surface, overhead vegetation, or stained water is much safer for them: the soft, angled light of dusk and dawn, safer yet. The hunting vision of predatory birds improves with higher contrast and brighter lighting. Noon on a summer day is often time for a nap in the shade; that is what the fish will be doing.

It is possible to have too little light also. When a stream is in the constant shadow of steep cliffs or impenetrable tree canopy, plant growth and productivity will decline.

Insect hatches too are affected by temperature and light, and when insects are hatching, fish are feeding. Insects are poikilotherms like fish and water temperature is the chief trigger for their maturation. When temperatures are comfortable, hatches are generally best: too cold and the only activity will be from larval forms underwater, too hot and hatches diminish because of the dry air. Insect wings dry too quickly when it's hot, preventing the emergence of nicely formed wings. This adverse effect of rapid drying is one reason hatches are more prominent on days when there is more humidity and also explains the preponderance of hatches on drizzly or snowy days. Getting a feel for the size and color of insect life by disturbing the streambed above a seine, by checking the rocks in the stream and the bushes along the bank, or simply by catching a spinner in your hat, is always time well spent.

Current and gradient also affect fish density. In higher-gradient mountain streams, fish might pile up in plunge pools, while slower streams, like meadow brooks, distribute fish more widely. As current steadies, cover becomes more important.

Taking time to observe the environment is finally the key to fish density and location. Temperature, cover, and current are the three biggest factors guiding your hunt.

## fly choice

The fish on small streams, say less than fifteen feet wide, are generally thought to be less finicky when it comes to eating a fly. I think this is true. Since most small streams are shallower, they can usually be fished with a dry fly almost exclusively in season. The fish will also tend to take a wide variety of flies because there are rarely large hatches (which turn trout into selective gourmets). Smaller waters only have a café menu: You can order anything as long as it's the blue plate special and you'd better decide fast. In small streams I often fish one generic surface or shallow fly.

This is not to say that wet flies, nymphs, or even streamers are not going to do better at times. When trout are deep in runs or down in the shadows of an undercut, subsurface flies are needed. Plunge pools are often better prospected with a deeper fly. Stained water or rough water precludes dries. And finally, if your dry is being ignored, it's rarely a bad idea to "go below." However, starting with a dry fly on most clear, small streams is a good strategy. More on choosing flies is covered later.

### approach

Small stream fish, which are more readily exposed to predators and with fewer places to hide, tend to be easily spooked, and will scatter at the wave of a rod or even the thump of a foot on a moss-covered embankment. Approach quietly and from downstream, maybe even crouching or crawling. (Kneepads do encourage stealth.) Use rocks and trees to camouflage your profile and movement, and remember to keep your head low when peering from behind. Stay in the shadows. Move slowly. Stealth takes time, as any hunter knows.

Casting from the bank without wading is an effective, if challenging, way to fish small streams. This kind of commando fishing is best done by sight fishing, when you can spot a trout on its lie. Stalk within range, keep your head down, and utilize streamside camouflage. When you can, reach the target with a bow and arrow cast. Even if part of your line will drape the bank or streamside rocks, take your shot. If you get a take, you can generally lift your line clear of streamside brush when the fish is on.

A more common approach is to wade carefully upstream, stopping at the outlet or tail of each pool. Hide behind any midstream rocks and stay low, then cast into the pool above. Try a couple casts to each side of the current, paying attention to eddies and obstructions. Send another couple of casts down the main tongue of current. Then move up the pool and repeat again. Longer pools may take several of these sequences to cover from tail to head.

Experienced small stream anglers will move quickly on to the next pool. It doesn't take long to effectively scout and fish water likely to be productive. Small stream fishing covers a lot of ground, but be prepared to spend time fishing the less accessible areas of the stream too. With no fly line or guides to snag, the tenkara rod can be used to push back small limbs to extend a drift, and with its ability to quickly collapse, there is almost no stream bank off limits. Other anglers often bypass these difficult spots, leaving untested fish for you.

Long runs and undercut banks should also be fished thoroughly. Cast and drift the close edge of the current, then down the current, and lastly try a cast against the bank. This order keeps you from spooking the closest fish. Again, keep as much line off the water as you can. The simple lob cast is very effective as you explore these runs.

Pocket water, the deeper water running through a huddle of larger rocks found in a cut or gorge, should be fished carefully. Tenkara, with its long reach, is ideal for fishing midstream boulders. An overhead or side-arm cast into the triangle of smoother water downstream, followed by a cast to each side, and finally flicked into the cushion (upstream water) that surrounds each likely rock or boulder, is needed to fish pockets well. Cast a couple of times to each spot, ensuring that the fish has seen the offering. Fishing pocket water involves a very quick presentation. Pockets may require a nymph or wet fly if they're especially deep.

## fly presentation

Where and how to place a fly are essential to fishing a small stream well. Accurate casting starts with the planning of fly placement. There is only one best place from which to cast to a lie or rise. In the small stream, inches can make the difference. Before you cast, try to visualize the fly landing, leading the fish, and settling into a natural drift. Concentration ensures accuracy.

Trout vision is limited above the water surface to a ninety-seven-degree cone, called Snel's Circle. Beyond this cone, refraction becomes reflection and the surface becomes a mirror that the fish cannot see through, a reason to stay low when approaching. What's less well known is that because of the refraction and bending of light near the edge of the circle, there is a magnification (almost two times) of anything on the surface, giving trout a close-up of your fly, especially those small flies. Furthermore, this magnification spotlights the top of the fly first as it drifts into view, giving some importance to its wings or upper profile. The diameter to the edge of Snel's Circle is a little more than the depth of the fish; in other words, if a fish is a foot deep, the diameter of the circle is around fourteen inches.[1]

Trout have a thirty-degree blind spot behind and a thirty-degree limit on their stereoscopic (binocular) vision in front. They are also nearsighted. This means approaching from behind (from downstream) is the stealthiest. Furthermore, fish are going to feed primarily in the small binocular cone in front of their noses.

Enhanced light reception allows fish to see in much darker conditions than you or I can. Their peripheral vision (aided by the vibration-sensing lateral line) allows them to pick up movement at quite a distance. Trout can see color as well, though reds and yellows fade with depth and surface color tends to be grayed and less intense underwater.

Subtle motion and the profile of a fly can attract a fish's attention from a distance, but the final decision often takes place within inches. A fish will first approach and turn toward the fly based on surface or light disturbance. The distance it will move depends on water temperature and food scarcity. For a closer look it will position the fly within its binocular vision and, if the fly's on the surface, at the edge of Snel's Circle. Unnatural movement or drag will cause the fish to turn away.

If conditions allow, a fish will cautiously approach on a rise before taking a fly. For this reason, imitative, natural-looking flies are often needed in clear and quiet water. The close-up is the final audition before a take.

A fly's size and coloration are important when a fish has time for a close-up, but a good presentation is still the number one criteria for enticing a fish to bite. If a trout cannot see a fly with clarity until it approaches, the movement or profile of the fly is what will trigger its interest. Brighter-colored attractor flies are fine in faster water.

Insects dimple the surface and wiggle a little, but dragging a fly with a speedboat wake will frighten fish. Dragging a fly is perhaps the most common error in presentation. On the other hand, with a wet fly or streamer, a little bit of pulsing movement will imitate attempts at propulsion. Likewise a crawling or tumbling nymph may lift and fall while drifting along the bottom.

Tenkara's sidearm cast can naturally create an upstream belly in the line, very useful for preventing drag. Such a cast across the body to the left leaves a curve of line to the same side, which is good when flow is from that direction. The same cast to the right leaves a belly of line to the right. This is very useful in casting a dry fly as the belly lies across the

faster currents, adding many seconds to your drift on longer casts before straightening out.

Mostly, though, tenkara anglers try to keep as much line as possible suspended off the water. The ability to keep line off the water is the greatest advantage of tenkara fishing. As someone new to tenkara, suspending your line in a shallow "j" or catenary curve is one of the skills you will need to practice. If you are used to fishing small streams with a western rod, you are going to love this ability to keep most of your line off the water even while having a longer reach. Drag is much easier to prevent with the long arm of a tenkara rod.

The quiet time spent planning an approach, the careful upstream wade, and the "soft eyes" used to catch all the nuances of water movement are, in my experience, very meditative experiences. Medical research has shown that such quiet enhances the connections in a section of the brain known as the pre-frontal region. This region is responsible for keeping the balance between internal chaos and boredom; it enables goal setting and planning, allows us to listen to our intuition, and improves the clarity of our moral compasses. We refer to these capabilities as executive functions. Only human beings have this section of the brain. Silencing the ego through quiet concentration is known to enhance the neurological connections that serve these functions.

### the retrieve

Our planning has been good and our presentation has the softness of a landing mayfly. How do we retrieve the fly in a tempting fashion that will help stimulate a reluctant fish to bite?

The most common retrieve is none at all . . . the dead drift. The fly is allowed to move at the speed of the current. Monitor its progress by comparing the fly or indicator to nearby foam or leaves. Keep as much of the line as possible off the water and focus on the area around it. At the end of the cast lift the line off the water as carefully as possible, well away from your target area. The dead drift is the single most effective small stream retrieve. Don't try others until the dead drift fails.

Dead drifting is usually done in an upstream direction to avoid contrary currents and to present a longer, drag-free drift. However downstream drifting is possible too. Simply drop the fly on the water and lower the tip to give it slack as it floats away. Downstream dead drifts require awareness of contrasting currents as well, keeping as much line off the water as possible.

The downstream drift is useful for directing a fly into a particularly brushy spot or a feeding lane that would be unreachable with a cast. A fly can simply drift downstream under the low branches. Remember that with a downstream dead drift you are now facing the fish rather than coming at it from behind. Crouching or kneeling becomes even more important to avoid presenting an easily seen profile.

At the end of a drift, and if the water is relatively slow, let the fly drag slightly; work it a little with an alternating tug and release of a few inches. This little skate on the surface or pulsing below can often stimulate a hit by a fish that has been curiously following your fly. He won't want to see his dinner get away.

You can also add movement during the drift. A little motion can prevent too close a look at an imitation, catch the eye of slumbering fish, and help stimulate a strike when drifting won't work. Fish often respond well to imitative motion. In general, keep the motion subtle and understated, although on rare occasions a larger movement can stimulate an aggressive, territorial strike. Tenkara, with its long reach, short line, and very fine tip, gives far more control over the retrieve than western fly fishing. This control allows for very small movements of your fly. This can be just the trick to tempt a fish.

The traditional *sakasa kebari,* or reverse hackle fly, is fished with a pulsing tip motion that flares the hackle tips of the fly in a seductive manner. Cast upstream of your target, and give the fly time to sink a bit. Send three or four pulses to the fly while retrieving it in the upper six inches of water. Then recast. This is the traditional Japanese tenkara presentation. Pulsing your rod tip very slightly is all that is needed. This retrieve is often started with a relatively hard landing; such a cast attracts attention to the

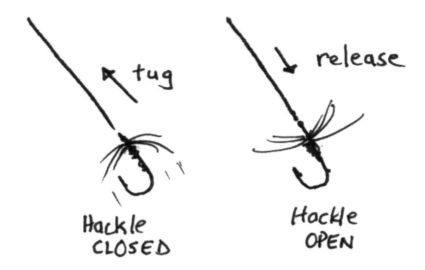

**tug**

**release**

**Hackle CLOSED**

**Hackle OPEN**

fly and tucks the fly below the surface tension. Very effective in riffled water, this retrieve and cast is a fun way to test a faster stream. However, it can be surprisingly effective even in quiet water where a softer landing and subtle movement are more typical. It is a more active form of casting than most western fly fishermen are accustomed to, but it encourages the testing of a lot of water very quickly.

Varying the twitches of a dry fly in still water can sometimes get the attention of a nearby fish, stimulating a strike. On the other hand, restraint and long stretches of stillness may also do the trick. Patience is one of the primary defenses of nature and one of the weaknesses of the unsuccessful angler.

Japanese anglers have a strategy for working hesitant fish, which is called *sutabari.* It roughly means "to show the fly." By placing a couple casts near your target you can interest the fish, then stimulate a bite by putting the fly right in his feeding lane. Western literature calls this "manufacturing a hatch." Give a targeted fish or a prime lie a couple good presentations before changing strategies.

Occasionally, the skittering of dry flies across the water surface will also entice a reluctant fish. Use the rod tip to keep the fly flitting lightly from one spot to another. It is hard for a fish to resist but can also result in many missed bites.

Working longer runs with a nymph or kebari can be a lot of fun. Lob the fly upstream and lead it through the run with as much line off the water as you can manage. Watch the line carefully. Lift and drop it a bit through the run. Cast well above the fishy spots so the fly has time to get deeper.

When retrieving with a tenkara rod use your imagination. Try different tempos. If you are an active angler you are going to like the variety of retrieves tenkara offers. Trust your hunches and be creative. This can often result in strikes that are otherwise hard to explain.

Whether you are fishing a meandering meadow stream or churning pocket water in a gorge, tenkara allows you to interact with the water in ways that would otherwise be difficult if not impossible. Explore these treasured spaces with your intuition. Allow yourself time to be absorbed. Observe closely and give yourself over to the sound of the stream, the smells of the undergrowth, the warmth of the sun, the chill of a mountain breeze. The effective hunter becomes one with his surroundings and can begin to sense his prey.

---

## Sources from Pages 69-79

1. Harmon, Robert, and Cline, John, "At the Edge of the Window," *Fly Rod and Reel,* March 1980.

# CHAPTER 8

# large water

KEEP CLOSE TO NATURE'S HEART . . . AND BREAK CLEAR AWAY ONCE IN AWHILE, AND CLIMB A MOUNTAIN OR SPEND A WEEK IN THE WOODS. WASH YOUR SPIRIT CLEAN.

—John Muir

On a recent trip to a Rocky Mountain lake above tree line, I felt compelled to pack in my western five-weight as well as my tenkara rod. I was worried that the limited reach of my thirteen-foot tenkara rod wouldn't be able to effectively fish such a large lake, especially since there was no tree cover along its shore. I shouldn't have worried. I ended up using the tenkara rod almost exclusively and caught plenty of cutthroat and lake trout. In a week I had only two fish break off and I landed an eighteen-inch "cut" on 5X tippet. What a blast!

Large waters can be fished effectively with tenkara, though you will be limited in your reach and in the size of the fish you can land. Mostly it requires rethinking how you fish. Start by imagining the water divided into smaller reachable sections. Plan to fish the sections as if they were smaller water. Where are the prime lies? Where do I need to be to fish it and how do I approach?

The chutes that enter or drain lakes can be very productive fishing locations; food is concentrated at inlets and outlets and fish congregate on the flats to either side. This part of a lake is generally easy to approach and is nearly always the location most likely to contain feeding fish.

Drop-offs and points can be fished with tenkara too. These areas offer fish a place to retreat and hide quickly even while presenting more fecund beds for feeding. These shallows are warmed by the sun early in the season and early in the day, allowing you to fish when the rest of a lake is "asleep." If there is a choice, fish the leeward side of a lake; wind often pushes the warmer surface layers and drifting insects in that direction.

In lakes with weed beds, fishing the openings and along the current breaks can be aided by the long reach of a tenkara rod. With very small openings you can actually drop a fly in these patches, something you might not reach with a short rod. Never forget, fish concentrate at the "edges," the areas most effectively prospected with tenkara, even on lakes.

Tenkara rods are a lot of fun from a float tube too, a method of fishing that opens up most of the rest of the shoreline and the drop-offs. Because you are low to the water, the long tenkara rod helps clear your cast much better than a short rod. In a windy environment, a heavier, level line (say, a seventeen-pound fluorocarbon) will usually be more effective than a furled line. Keep your flipper movements subtle and slow or you will start to miss the longer reach of a western rod. The lateral line of a fish is very sensitive to water pressure waves.

Bigger rivers can be fished with tenkara rods too. Just think of the river as being divided into several small streams. Keep your focus close at hand and move patiently. Fish the bank and the pocket water. Don't forget to use a wading staff in heavier water. It is always a good idea to wade by quartering upstream in a river you don't know. If you start to get in deeper than you'd like, you can back down with the current rather than getting in a predicament fighting the current. Keep your wading belt snug in big water too. A fall in faster streams can be dangerous, especially if you fill your waders with icy water. As mentioned before, shin guards keep your wader legs tight and allow for easier wading.

Bottom prospecting big river runs is not much different than in small streams. Cast upstream and lead your nymph or streamer like a dog on a leash. Keep that rod tip high and as much of the line off the water as you can. Using a fluorocarbon tippet with a smaller diameter will help you get down deep; small diameters sink quicker. For years, Joe Humphries, author and Penn State instructor, has recommended using untapered monofilament for nymphing. He's right . . . although casting a fluorcarbon level line with a tenkara rod is easier than with the western rig.

A jigging motion for a bottom-bouncing, weighted nymph is also very productive in streams with deeper runs. Enough weight should be used

to get the fly down to the productive six to twelve inches where fish tend to hover. Lifting slightly and dropping the nymph through the length of a cast will often be too much for a fish to ignore.

The tenkara rod makes a very nice Euro-nymphing rod too, though it needs to be handled differently. Euro nymphing (also called Czech nymphing, but originating with the Polish and modified by the Spanish and French, etc.) involves casting a brace of nymphs upstream, actively leading them through the target area (usually thought of in grids), and then lifting downstream with a bit of wrist roll. Sometimes the upper nymph (or middle, if there are three) is purposely weighted more than the point nymph. This arrangement gets the brace deep but allows the point fly to hover above the bottom. With three flies the top fly is the lightest of the three and either hovers in the middle depths or can be used at the surface to "dib," or bounce on the surface. In fast and deep water, the flies are heavily weighted, the classic Czech nymph. When water is shallow, even as little as a foot deep, lighter nymphs are used, often with the point fly being heavier. Euro nymphing is wrongly assumed to be just about lobbing heavy braces of nymphs. However, casting more than one fly does take a slower and gentler cast in order to prevent tangles. When Euro nymphing, a tight line enhances detection of nibbles. A downstream lift also adds to your chances. The frequent use of Euro nymphing by competitive fly anglers speaks to its effectiveness.

The sensitivity of the tenkara rod is ideal for this kind of nymphing, though generally favoring lighter weighted flies. Indicators are rarely needed, though can be helpful for beginners. A colorful bit of mono or a small section Dacron reel backing is a common choice. In the chapter on making lines I'll show you a couple of tricks.

Dry flies on larger rivers can be fished upstream very effectively, just as on small streams. It is even more important to recognize the feeding lanes on a larger stream, though. Land your fly above the suspected lie so that it dead-drifts right to your target. Spots in the river where two currents join are likely holding water. Fish often won't move as far to chase a fly on larger water.

Fishing dry flies downstream on larger water is much more effective than on small streams. In fact, downstream fishing on larger streams can be more productive than fishing up, something that is almost never true on small streams. Why? First, it is easier to wade downstream if there is a significant current and you know the water. Second, you can slide your fly across the surface more easily into suspected feeding lanes and under branches, taking advantage of the current. In broken water and pockets, this can be very effective. Though a fish's vision may be limited in larger water, remember to keep your profile blended with streamside vegetation and your movements subtle. Crouching lower, even in a big river, can improve fishing.

If a bigger river is discolored with runoff, and if nothing is biting, don't forget to use a little larger fly and give it some motion. Streamers shine here. Fishing a tributary or a backwater can be a good high water strategy. When a river is high, it can still be fished. Just remember that high water concentrates fish in the slower moving boundaries, often right up against the bank or deep on the bottom. Also, even the smallest obstructions provide a welcome break from faster water.

Float tubes in a slower river can be a blast too. Fish the edges of the lazy water and just pick up the tube and walk if it gets too shallow. (Float tubes are not recommended for faster rivers because they can be dangerous.) A great smallmouth river near my home offers a shuttle service for tubers. For a few bucks you can ride all day. Prepare for some questions about your "funny" rod though.

And speaking of warm waters, I enjoy fishing for bluegill, red-eyes, and smallmouth almost as much as trout. Warm water fish are all you get on some rivers, and in late summer it is often easier to find smallmouth than trout. These tepid-water survivors can be as aggressive as any rainbow. If fishing for warm water species, poppers and streamers are, of course, very productive. I really enjoy the surface smack of a bream on a sparse dry too, but a suspended nymph is more productive for the bigger sunfish. Sound and vibration are more important in this kind of fishing; fish often identify their supper with the lateral line of sensitive nerve endings.

Night fishing on bigger water for both warm and cold water fish can be very exciting with short tenkara lines. I feel more in touch with a tenkara line at night than longer western fly lines, and seem to get in much less trouble. Be prepared for bigger fish, and for safety's sake you should have a thorough daytime knowledge of any nighttime fishing spots.

I have a delightful twelve-foot Kevlar canoe that weighs only twenty-two pounds. Such a lightweight canoe matches perfectly with a tenkara rod. I can portage into areas that are rarely fished and have the day to myself. My rod and fly box slip into my pocket, my lunch goes in a fanny pack, and I wear my life vest which pads my shoulders on the carry in.

When canoeing, threading the uppermost guide of a western rod is awkward. In contrast telescoping a tenkara rod is a breeze. It's a little thing, but I also like not having a reel banging around on the bottom of the canoe; tenkara rods are just quieter. Not to mention that being able to quickly collapse your rod is a great advantage during a brushy canoe adventure; emergency paddling with your rod tip caught in an overhanging limb can be dodgy.

Tenkara is not ideal for deep lake fishing, though jigging for crappie is not out of the question. Spiders or a weighted drop-fly over a brush pile of crappie can be hours of fun. Putting a couple nymphs under an indicator and allowing them to ride the wavelets across a lake shelf is a completely lazy way to fish from a canoe or pram. Some days I just want to relax.

Dapping a fly is a traditional Irish method of fishing across shallow lakebeds, and suited to tenkara rods. Simply use a heavily hackled fly and light line (a furled line is much preferred), allowing the fly to flit and lift over the surface as your boat drifts in the wind. This is a lovely imitation of hatching mayflies.

So you see, tenkara is not for small waters alone, though that is where it got its pedigree. When you think about it, most of your catches are within reach of a tenkara rod no matter the size of the water. In fact, longer casts with a western rod can sometimes make it difficult to hook up and play a fish. I think I miss more bites with longer casts too. If you think it might be tough to fish a larger body of water with tenkara, try it anyway. You might be as surprised as I was.

# CHAPTER 9

# hook to hand

EVERY BEAUTY WHICH IS SEEN HERE BELOW BY PERSONS OF PER-
CEPTION RESEMBLE MORE THAN ANYTHING ELSE THE CELESTIAL
SOURCE FROM WHICH WE ARE ALL COME.

—Michelangelo

Your approach has been well planned and stealthy. You've placed the fly in the fishiest spot in reach. Your patience pays off with a take, be it sudden or sipping. What now?

Set the hook strongly and quickly. Use your predator reflexes and some vigor. You don't need a large motion. After all, you don't want to end up with your rod tip in the trees above you. But use enough strength to transmit your striking force through the rod to the fish: a snap of the wrist and forearm. You can't be bashful with a tenkara rod.

A sideways motion will work too, although a side pull may require slightly more force as you have to overcome more water tension. Being able to strike quickly requires limiting the amount of slack. The cheery fly fishing greeting "tight lines" is just as important a reminder with tenkara.

A roll cast–type motion toward the fly can hook a fish too, but this will take some practice and control. This is worth trying when you have absolutely no overhead clearance. Flick your tip down and toward the fish with vigor. The tug of the line is enough to hook a fish if you've kept your hooks sharp.

If you are fast enough with one of these techniques, you have hooked your prey, and now the battle is on. With the exquisite touch offered by the tenkara rod, every tug and twist is transmitted to the grip. Even a very small fish will send motion down the rod. And when you tie into a larger one it's almost startling.

Keep tension on the line, but don't pull too tight. The tenkara rod is lithe, and will protect your tippet well. Allow the fish to work a bit without giving up total control. If it is a larger fish, be prepared to follow him downstream, staying even with him or below him. Keeping below makes him fight the current as well as you. Keep in contact with the fish but allow it to tire before trying to land it.

There's an old joke that says a fish breaks off "because of the jerk on the end." It is true, however, that sudden pulls are more likely to part your tippet than smoothly applied constant tension. When a fish jumps, drop the entire rod low to the water. The slack may protect the tippet. Most breakoffs are caused by too much tension rather than too little.

If you need to guide him away from snags and sharp rocks, do so with as light a touch as you can manage. Pulling his nose up sometimes makes him easier to lead. At this critical point, you're the middle man between the breaking strength of your tippet and the fish's urgency.

As a last resort, if he cannot be stopped or controlled, ease up all pressure. Sometimes this will fool him into making a wrong directional change in your favor. Then the fight can begin anew. This risks loosening the hook in the fish's mouth but can sometimes be effective. Once the fish is tired, it is easier to guide him away from his hideouts and toward your net.

In spite of the absence of a reel, you will find that bringing a fish to net with a tenkara rod is often both quicker and easier on the fish. There is no line-to-reel transfer and hence no lag time. Because the tip of the rod is further over the water, controlling the fish's nose is more likely with the additional leverage. And lastly, the give of the flexible tip keeps a more constant and tiring tension on the fish.

As the fish fatigues and approaches, keep your moves quiet and bring him to the net or hand gently. If you are going to release him, unhook him in the water if you can. Simply run your hand down to the line and twist the barbless hook loose. If you must handle him, wet your hands first and lift him onto his back or side, avoiding the lateral line (which has very sensitive nerve endings). Holding a net underwater to the side of your left leg is the best position to prepare for a net capture. Holding the tenkara rod high and perhaps a bit behind you helps to bring the fish headfirst into the net.

When attempting to land a larger fish, follow the fish by staying parallel with or below it. As he quiets, bring him toward you; if he begins to fight, give him room to run again. Drop your tip with any sudden runs.

Dr. Ishigaki talks about balancing two opposing forces in fighting a fish. These forces are *inasu* and *kawasu,* or weakness and strength. He explains that when the fish is strong, a fisherman should be weak in his handling of it. In other words, give line and use soft pressure. When the fish is weaker, use a stronger handling to bring him close for netting or release. This dualism of winning over resistance with gentleness, yet being strong in the face of weakness, is metaphorical for so many things in life.

When landing a fish with a longer level line (up to twice the length of the rod), you must hand gather the line. Extend your rod hand as high as you can behind you, pulling the line into range of your off hand. Once you have pinched the line, your off arm becomes the only "give" in the system. Keep your arm as loose as possible. Any sudden pulls by the fish will certainly break the tippet at this point unless you remain flexible. Using a net is a good idea with longer lines. Once you are "handing" the fish, set your rod down or put the butt of the rod inside your hip waders or under your arm. Use both hands now to land your prize.

If you wish to take a picture, something that never quite lives up to the memories in my view, do so quickly in the net or water; this is healthier for the fish and makes a much better picture. There is something disturbing about a fish photographed against grass or gravel, even if handled carefully. Perhaps a few words in a notebook make for the best record, recording the memory as well as the conditions and technique.

Removing the hook is usually not hard. You can simply grab the fly and give it a push and twist at the same time. If you are using barbless hooks, this method will usually work. If the hook is more firmly embedded, use your hemostat to grab the fly as close to the bend as you can. Again a push and twist is all that is needed.

Deep hooking is rare with tenkara, as it is with traditional fly fishing. The number one cause of deep hooking is live bait. Deep hooks should not be removed but left in place. Bronze hooks will typically dissolve over several weeks. If a hook must be left in the fish, its feeding ability will be aided by leaving a small length of tippet (a few inches) attached to the hook.[1] The variables most associated with mortality after release, in order, are: live bait, deep hooking, high air or water temperature, extended play, and barbed hooks.[2]

You've done it. You've pitted yourself against the wiles of one of nature's most exquisitely adapted animals. You've tapped into one of the basic instincts of all humans, the predatory instinct to hunt food. You've spent time stepping out of the contrived and constructed and into the natural rhythms of wildness, unexplored by most people. Perhaps a moment to give thanks would be a good thing. If a lifetime is made of its memories, savor this one.

### Sources from Pages 87-91

1. Bauer, Daryl, correspondence, Nebraska Game and Parks Commission, September 2007.
2. Bartholomew, Aaron, Review in *Fish Biology and Fisheries,* February 2005.

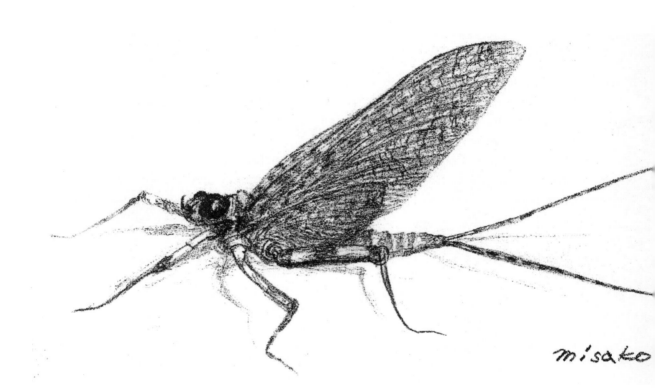

misako

# bugs 101

ONLY THOSE WITH PATIENCE TO DO SIMPLE THINGS PERFECTLY WILL
ACQUIRE THE SKILL TO DO DIFFICULT THINGS EASILY.

—Johann Schiller

Aquatic and terrestrial insects are on the menu for any trout stream. Observing the chef's special will go a long way toward enticing fish to your fly. Sampling the brush with your hat, and the water and bottom with a seine or fish-tank net, can bring you samples. I stretch a simple cheesecloth bag over my fishing net, and then stir up a little of the streambed and lift a few rocks upstream. If you haven't tried sampling a stream bottom, I think you'll be surprised. You don't even have to know what the insects are, just the location, size, shape, and color.

Aquatic insects go through such a predictable lifecycle that hatches can often be predicted by date and even hour. Furthermore, each insect prefers a specific temperature, light, and humidity to trigger its hatches. In early spring, hatches (and hence fish feeding) don't begin until the water warms up. Later in the season, as a general rule, the heat of midday shuts hatches down. A degree of air humidity allows insect wings to dry a bit slower and is preferred by the emerging adults or duns. Hatches therefore are often most prolific on cloudy days, and near dusk or dawn.

Depending on the water type, late summer fly choices are typically biased toward the terrestrials, including ants, beetles, and grasshoppers. This is especially true in streams with depths that vary with rain runoff and that border grassy fields and meadows or have a lot of overhanging brush.

Tailwaters often favor the tiny chironomids, or midges, which hatch in abundance from this water. The water temperature is stable and the water fertile. Yet studies have shown that it is the midge's ability to survive the drying out periods and wide variations in water depth that most favors them in these waters.

The weed beds of lakes and streams may harbor freshwater shrimp and scuds, as do tailwaters with lots of aquatic vegetation. Likewise, feeder fish stay near cover and prefer shallows.

Some anglers make such a serious study of insects that they rival professional entomologists. "Matching the hatch" is a time-honored approach to dry and emerger fly fishing. A little knowledge of insect prevalence can't help but improve your fishing, whether you are matching a quilled dun or just making whatever fly you have on hand skitter a bit in imitation. When sampling, choose the most active and most frequent insect specimens to imitate.

The following pages contain a very brief guide to identifying common aquatic insects to get you started:

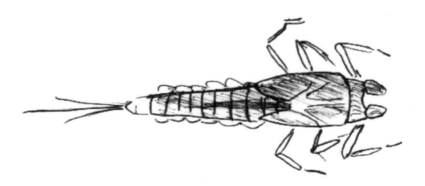

**Mayfly nymphs** usually have three tails (though some have two), but always have gills along the side of the abdomen. Mayfly nymphs range from 3 to 16 millimeters long and cannot tolerate pollution or high temperatures. They swim with a quick, porpoise-like motion. Colors include black, gray, and brown, with dark wing pads prominent over the thorax.

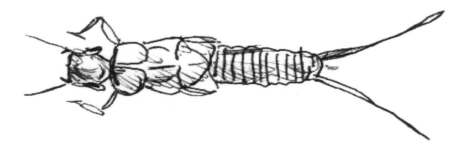

**Stonefly nymphs** are generally large nymphs growing up to 60 millimeters. They have two long tails that they retain as adults and two prominent antennae. Their gills are on the thorax below the legs like hairy armpits. These clumsy-looking nymphs climb on streamside rocks to mature. Their oxygen needs are great and they require fast water without pollution or silt, thus their presence indicates excellent water quality. Most are shiny brown or black but can be light tan.

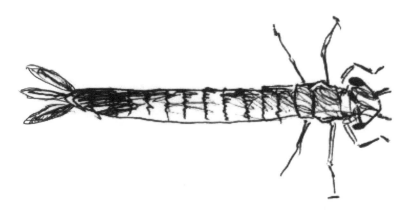

**Damselfly nymphs** are easy to identify with their three large paddle-shaped gills at the tail end, which they often wiggle to help oxygenate. Their large compound eyes are prominently black against their brownish body. Their grasping jaws help these carnivores grasp their prey.

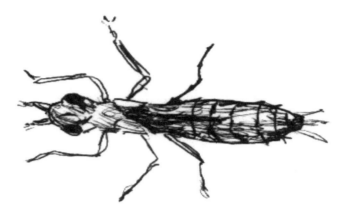

**Dragonfly nymphs** are jet powered, expelling water for squirt propulsion. Brown or olive, these large (20–50 millimeter) wide flat nymphs molt on streamside vegetation and boat docks. They have prominent compound eyes and are found in aquatic vegetation where there are slow currents.

**Caddisfly larvae** look like small caterpillars, varying from brown to chartreuse to cream, usually with a darker head and shoulder. Many make protective cases from tiny gravel and vegetation, and some make web-like nets to catch food. They are tolerant of warmer water.

**Midge larvae,** also called chironomids, are tiny, wormlike, thin, and segmented. The red ones are especially tolerant of lower oxygen levels because they have a compound like hemoglobin, so they can be found in silt. Their darker gut-line can usually be seen, especially in the light green and clear larvae. They are very active, wiggling the ends together, burrowing into river mud and the bottom of ponds.

**Snails** of course are not insects at all but are gastropods. They are present in quiet water, especially on lakeside vegetation where they are common meals. Snails whose "door" opens to the left (with cone point up) have lungs, which tolerate oxygen-poor and organically thick water. Those that open to the right (illustrated) have gills, which require cleaner and better-oxygenated water. Left=lung=lousy.

**Scuds,** commonly called freshwater shrimp, are another invertebrate that swims rapidly on their side. They are mostly clear but pick up the color of their scavenged food: tan, pink, and green. They live in the aquatic vegetation of calm water.

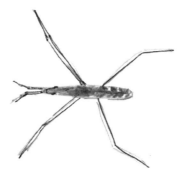

**Water striders** have tiny grooves in the legs that allow them to easily walk on water. They cannot detect movement above or directly below them so they are easily observed and are easy prey for fish. They can detect surface vibration easily, however, and locate food this way.

The **dobsonfly nymph,** or hellgrammite, is large and easily identified by its pinchers and armored appearance. Living between rocks, it preys on other insect larvae. Both the larvae and adult are nocturnal but are attracted by lights, with the adult often growing to five inches in length.

**Mayfly adults** have two stages: duns, when wings are a dull opaque and have a mottled appearance, and spinners, when the wings are translucent and lighter colored. Hatches enable large masses of mayflies to mate quickly, as the adults live only a day or two and do not feed at all.

**Caddisfly adults** look like moths in their fluttering flight. They are attracted to light, so they can be seen around dock lights and streamside cabin windows. Adults live for weeks and can mate several times. Females deposit eggs on the water surface and streamside vegetation, though some submerge, "gluing" their eggs to the bottom gravel and staying below up to thirty minutes.

**Alderfly adults** look very similar in size and wing position to the caddisfly, but can be distinguished by its shorter antennae and darker coloration. It lives on stream side brush, and is a much poorer flyer. Its nymph has a single "tail."

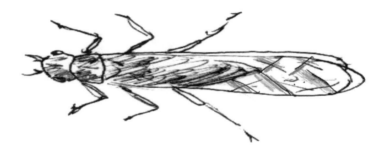

**Stonefly adults** are clumsy fliers looking a little like dragonflies in flight. Their wings fold flat against their back and the veins give the appearance of a hair braid at rest. You see stoneflies in the book and movie *A River Runs Through It.*

**Aquatic moths** are important evening and night foods fluttering actively along stream banks. Their cream to tan colored delta wings leave dusty scales if captured.

**Midge adults** are small, prolific insects that can be found year-round. They comprise a surprisingly large percentage of fish diets. They often are seen in mating clusters on the water surface, and can be present in large numbers. They can often be seen covering streamside vehicles (they have a predisposition toward white and yellow paint).

# CHAPTER 11

# kebari and western flies

GOD NEVER DID MAKE A MORE CALM, QUIET, AND INNOCENT RECRE-
ATION THAN ANGLING.

—Izaak Walton

**To fish effectively,** most anglers will find a dozen or so flies that work consistently, and keep gravitating back to them. A few professional fly fishermen use a single fly design. Western fly fisherman Rim Chung, for instance, likes his own emerger design, the RS2. Tenkara fisherman Dr. Hisao Ishigaki fishes a simple reverse hackle fly. The very best fly fishermen learn how to use a few flies well. Keeping your fly selection simple makes on-the-water decisions easier and is in keeping with the ease of tenkara fishing. It is tempting to start by buying a number of different flies when you are a beginner, but you will find yourself simplifying later. Why not start with just a few proven designs and learn their history, their uses, and how best to present them? Better yet, tie your own.

## fly tying

Tying your own flies is not difficult, and catching fish on flies you've made yourself adds a whole new level of enjoyment to the sport. After factoring in the time spent, you might not be saving much over discount house flies, but the ones you make for yourself are usually of better quality. You might even decide to tweak the standard designs to come up with your own unique "magic" fly. Fly tying can be a very enjoyable hobby unto itself.

You can start tying flies with very little investment. Given that specialty tenkara flies may not be readily available at your local tackle dealer, it makes sense to start tying your own. If you make a fly or two following the instructions below, you can get a feel for fly tying and may want to spend another thirty to forty dollars on a vise and thread bobbin, the only two pieces of equipment really needed to tie flies regularly. This experiment is just to give you insight into fly tying, which is often viewed as difficult and esoteric. (You may not want to fish this first effort. If you do become a fly tyer you will appreciate saving your first fly.)

A traditional reverse hackle tenkara fly is one of the easier flies to tie, and since it can be fished as a dry fly or wet fly it is very versatile.

1. Clamp a bare hook (start with a #12 dry-fly hook) in your fly-tying vise. If you don't have a vise, clamp the hook in your hemostat and attach it firmly to the edge of a table using a C-clamp.

2. Collect a feather for your hackle. Hen hackle is fine but any small and thin feather collected in the yard will work. The barbs should be about one and a half times the width of the hook gape, the distance between shaft and barb. Pull off any fluff at the base of the feather and use your finger to fan the barbs slightly.

3. Tie ordinary sewing thread to the hook by wrapping the shaft of the hook with thread in one direction, then over-wrapping it back in the other direction. Hold the spool in the palm of your hand and direct the turns with your index finger and thumb. Trim off the tag. Cover the hook with thread to the point on the shaft where you want to place the hackle, usually one-third of the distance back from the eye. Avoid catching the barb by wrapping at a slight angle.

4. Now tie in the feather by holding the tip of the feather against the hook shaft, concave side up, and wrapping it with three or four tight turns of thread. Trim off the tip excess with scissors, and wrap thread over the trimmed tip to hide it. The thread on the eye side of the feather will represent the head, so feel free to add a little extra thread to shape. When done, wind the thread behind the feather attachment point toward the hook bend.

5. Now, holding the feather firmly and with constant tension (but not pulling too hard), wrap it four or five times around the hook shaft. The wraps should be very close together. This next is the hardest part and takes a little hand changing to keep it tight. While holding the turns firmly, tie the feather off behind (on the hook-bend side) by again over-wrapping the feather shaft with thread. Wrap it three times, then trim the excess feather. Keep it tight. A few extra turns over the excess hackle is done to hide the end.

6. Now pull the hackle, bending it with your thumb and three fingers, winding the thread tight against the wound feather hackle, over-wrapping it a bit so that the hackle tips point toward the hook eye. This leans the hackle forward in its distinctive reverse hackle position; the amount of lean is up to you. (See Misako's drawing at the beginning of the chapter.)

7. Finally, finish by wrapping thread around the hook shaft all the way to the bend of the hook. Then tie off your thread with several overhand knots. Cross the thread on itself with a twist of the fingers, placing the knot at the end of your thread wrap at the beginning of the hook bend, and pull it tight. Trim the thread closely. You can make it more secure with a dab of nail polish or waterproof Super Glue.

Interested in making your own flies regularly? A good bobbin (I recommend one with a ceramic tube that won't fray thread) is only ten to twenty dollars. A very usable vise can be had for not much more. The vise should hold a hook firmly and either have a heavy base or clamp to a table, nothing more. The ability to rotate is strictly optional.

Start by purchasing enough materials to make a couple of proven flies. Practice these before experimenting with your own designs. Buy hackle of good quality for dry flies; the so-called generic hackle is pre-sized and makes selection easy. There are many good books on fly tying and thousands of patterns are available online, many with easy to follow videos. It takes tying a dozen flies to learn a single pattern and to get a well-proportioned fly. Joining a "fly tie" session at a local fishing club is a way to get valuable critique and advance more quickly, as well as make friends. Fly tying can become an obsession unto itself, so be careful.

If you would rather purchase some of the traditional kebari flies, there are a few U.S. suppliers on the Web.

### fly choices

On most waters, the fly is less important than the presentation. However, you will be surprised by how often fish will have nothing to do with one fly but will be hungry for another. You will develop preferences as to how you like to fish, which will influence what flies you carry. Of course, the type of water you are fishing will influence your choices too.

Choosing a fly is part deduction and part guess. Early in the season I prefer larger and darker flies. "Dark flies on dark days" is a time-honored aphorism. There is a general progression, following the colors of spring, from gray-blue flies, to browns and olives, and finally chartreuse and yellows. Misako likes a bit of white at the eye end of her soft hackles. I often favor a small tag of green or red/orange on streamers and larger nymphs. Brighter and larger flies should be more effective in stained water while more natural-colored flies are used in clear water.

When you fish unfamiliar water, asking advice at a fly shop and then buying a half dozen of their recommended flies is always a good idea. Local knowledge should never be ignored.

Hiring a guide is almost always worth the investment. Tell the guide up front that you want to learn, not just fish, and she will help you tap into her own intimate experience with the local waters. Make clear to her that you are fishing with a tenkara rod, and what that means as far as reach. It may be the first time they have heard of tenkara.

What are my favorite flies? I have always been a sucker for buying and tying flies the "experts" think are the best, and so my preferences change like the weather. If you ask me the same question in a year, the answer is liable to be different. Fly preference seems to be based more on experi-

ence than science. For example, I asked four experienced tenkara anglers their favorite dry fly for mountain streams, and got four different answers. My West Coast consultant favors the Al Troth Elkhair Caddis. My Arkansas connection, the Fran Better's Usual. New York waters favored the Hans Weilenmann CDC and Elk, and in the Blue Ridge, Lee's Royal Wulff was praised. All are high-floating, easily seen flies, which may be their most important attribute. All work, and I believe these anglers would do nearly as well with any of the other choices.

Furthermore, most of my fly choices reflect my Blue Ridge and Appalachian home waters. When I fish out west my fly choices change. Your home waters may require something completely different in turn.

So when considering which flies to put in your arsenal, first think of how you will use them and what they will represent. Then simplify your selection as much as you can. Don't carry so many flies that you will get confused on the stream and spend more time changing flies than fishing.

## seasonal fly choice and strategies

When I am fishing late winter/early season water, I favor nymphs and streamers. I like a weighted Gold-ribbed Hare's Ear, the Zebra Midge Nymph, and Woolly Buggers in black and purple. I will often fish a Bugger followed by a nymph, a great searching strategy on medium-sized waters. Because colder water makes fish sluggish, you must fish the bottom slowly and expect subtle bites. Generally, an indicator is needed to do this well.

As the days warm up I start to experiment more with dry flies and emergers. When water temperatures warm to 50 degrees you'll see me trying a Parachute Adams, Royal Wulff, and Elkhair Caddis. A Partridge and Orange wet or sakasa kebari (brown on black or grizzly on red work best for me) are fun wet fly additions and imitate emergers on the Jackson River. If I fail to see rises, it's back to nymphing, now with faster sinking bead-heads. The Red Squirrel and Olive Bead-head are my favorites, though I add a thread "vein" on the dorsum for luck when I tie them. A tiny Zebra Midge under a dry fly indicator is my standard tailwater combination in spring, except in faster water where I might use two nymphs.

May is the best month for fishing in the Blue Ridge. Often I begin fishing the lighter colors, like the Yellow Comparadun or the X-caddis in tan and amber. These flies tend to be smaller though, as I work the Smith River hatches. My favorite streams are the small mountain streams like Whitetop Laurel and Big Wilson, where I favor Royal Wulffs and Gulpers.

Summer will see me fishing a Hi-viz Ant pattern, a Black Closed Cell Foam Beetle, and a Madam X Hopper. An Orange Stimulator shows up later in August while a Griffith Gnat and red or black midge patterns are still working on tailwaters such as the South Holston.

Late summer and early fall I generally target smallmouth bass with surface poppers, Woolly Buggers, and hellgrammite imitations. I like the relaxed float of the Gala to Glen Wilton section of the James River, though I'll admit the largest smallmouth are in the New River, especially near the armory and the Eggleston to Pembroke section.

Sunfishing with a Bully's Bluegill Spider is a great fly for fishing brush piles, especially around the head of Philpott Lake and while floating Fairy

Stone in my canoe. Pond fishing with a popper makes for guaranteed action, especially important when I take my seven-year-old nephew.

Remember that patterns are not as important as presentation. When fishing a pattern, give it a fair trial in a few different spots before changing. Last-minute refusals should be answered with a smaller version.

I must conclude with a reminder. Since tenkara is so new in the United States and Europe, the many adaptations of tenkara are still being explored. Dr. Ishigaki, the most recognized master of tenkara, fishes one pattern in several sizes and colors. Maybe we should take a page from his book. Indeed, a tenkara traditionalist may be dismayed at my mentioning so many western flies. In any case, find out what works best for you on your waters, and let me know. However, in the spirit of tenkara, do try to keep it simple.

# CHAPTER 12

# making tenkara lines

IN EVERY WALK WITH NATURE ONE RECEIVES FAR MORE THAN HE
SEEKS.

—John Muir

In all honesty, making your own lines is not really necessary. Furled commercial lines fish nicely right off the spool and level line fluorocarbon can just be cut to length. Both give satisfactory results, and I am slow to recommend any complication.

If you like to have control over every aspect of your fishing, however, or are an unrepentant tinkerer, making your own lines is the least expensive option, and can be fun to boot. Perhaps through your experimenting you may just come up with the next innovation in lines. You can certainly more closely adjust a line for the casting characteristics you prefer if you make your own. Besides, furled and fluorocarbon lines are really quite easy to make.

## furled lines

Furled lines are commonly made out of monofilament or thread. Almost any fiber that is not "furry" can be used, with fluorocarbon and nylon monofilament, and polyester and nylon thread, dominant. Nylon monofilament is close to neutrally buoyant and doesn't require floatant. Fluorocarbon sinks. Polyester thread lines are limper and allow more delicate presentations, which can be very useful for dry flies, while nylon monofilament is stiffer. Coating thread lightly with non-silicone floatant or floor wax will help it float. I have a slight bias toward nylon since it floats nicely without any treatment. Our ancestors fished furled lines made of horsehair, and there are a few tenkara anglers that still prefer it, though it tends to be heavier and more fragile.

The choice of color of furled lines is unlimited. Since most of the line will be held off the water, a highly visible, even fluorescent material can be chosen. This is the line I use when I teach, as it is much easier for eyes to follow. I really don't think the fish mind either, since they likely see more the shadow of the line than the color. However, I usually use a quieter color for my own lines, favoring a pale green or amber.

When you make a furled line, you simply join loops of monofilament or thread that are several feet long. The loops are then furled or twisted together to form a multi-strand line. By decreasing the number of loops as you proceed toward the tip of your line, you are able to form a taper that rolls and extends over the water nicely, carrying the fly.

To keep the loops even, you first need to set up a furling board. Any board that's 10 percent longer than the eventual length of line will do. At one end firmly screw in two large cup hooks or L hooks, then space out alternating pegs made from a dowel or broom handle. I use one-inch dowels and simply cut one-inch holes with a spade- or spur-point drill bit into a piece of scrap two-by-six, fourteen feet long. The dowels, cut to four inches, snug down in the drilled holes. This allows me to remove the dowels when I am ready to wind a leg or store the furling jig. A light sanding of any rough spots prevents unintentional snags; painting or lacquering is definitely optional, though a light, flat paint does make it a little easier to see the thread. The spacing of dowels will determine the gradient of your taper, and some ingenious furling boards have been made that allow the

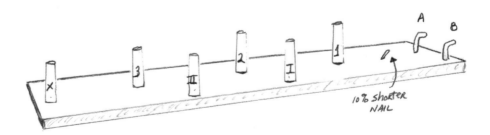

dowels to be adjusted. If you want you can spend a lot of time calculating different tapers and adjusting your line. The previous illustration (page 112) shows how I spaced my pegs for a twelve-foot furled line.

On leg A, dowels are fixed at 42, 81, and 113 inches. On leg B, they are at 64 and 98 inches. The tip dowel, X, is twelve feet from the L hooks.

To reiterate the general idea, you start at hook A and begin wrapping loops: several around peg 1, a few around 2, a couple around 3, and finally less as you go around X. Then on your way back up leg B, do the reverse, building taper rather than decreasing it. After both sides are done, wind each leg individually. Once under the tension of these windings, by putting the two legs together and unwinding, the magic of furling takes place with the two legs forming a beautifully simple, two-strand line.

### furling directions

1. Tie a simple overhand loop a couple inches long and place it over the anchor hook A. This small knot will not be noticeable, as it is wound within the line. It is actually better to have the loop a little long so the knot does not occur too close to the end, and of course it is easier, too. If you make this loop extra long you are essentially adding to the taper of the butt section, which is not a bad idea.

2. Make five loops back and forth between the nearest dowel #1 and anchor hook A. Don't worry if they overlap. Placing them far enough down the dowel that they are secure, but not so far down that they are difficult to slide off the dowel in latter steps, is the ticket.

3. On the next half loop from the anchor hook go past the dowel #1 to dowel #2. It doesn't matter whether you pass inside or out. Whichever way you started is fine.

4. Go around dowel #2 then back to dowel #1, but pass the whole spool in between the first five leg loops as you go around. This

is what locks the loops together. Some recommend tugging the loop down a bit, but I don't think it is necessary, just be consistent. You want your loops of each segment to be about the same size. Now take your spool back down around dowel #2 and back up and through dowel #1 loop again. Do this three times total. Now you have two segments of five and three loops respectively, joined together at dowel #1.

5.  Do the same for dowel #2 to dowel #3, but using only two loops this time.

6.  Now pass from dowel #3 around the tip dowel X up to dowel II on leg B. You are using dowel X simply to turn the corner at this step. This loop must go on the outside of dowel X of course, no matter where you have been turning loops, inside or outside. Go around dowel II either side, and go back past the tip dowel X and back up to dowel #3 on side A, going through the loop again.

7.  Now back around the tip dowel X and up past dowel II to dowel I. This will give you a simple three-strand tip when legs A and B are combined.

8.  After going around dowel I, loop back down to II, going through the loop to bind it. Finally make five loops between dowel I and hook B.

9.  End by tying another overhand loop just long enough to reach the cup hook with tension. The thread or mono will give a little with tension so tie it a bit short rather than a bit long.

10. Now clamp the strands beneath a clamp on the tip dowel X so the two legs A and B can be wound separately. Any kind of easy-to-apply clamp will work, but don't injure the thread. (This is an important step. I have seen other furlers try to extend out

one leg and attempt to wind the whole thing at once, which is unbelievably unwieldy with a twelve-foot line. Others make the two legs separate, which I think just takes more time.)

11. Carefully lift all the loops off the dowels on leg A (in my rig I just remove the dowels). With a cup hook mounted firmly in the chuck of a power drill, transfer the loops from leg A and begin winding. Wind until the cord is shortened by the twisting to just past the 10 percent nail (fourteen inches or so). Some folks time the winding, but I think just estimating the 10 percent shortening is fine. The two legs have to be close to the same winding tension, but not exactly. Place a paper clip through the loop on the drill cup hook and hang it on the nail. Transferring the loops from the cup hook to the paper clip is easy, though occasionally you need to back twist with your fingers a tiny bit to open a loop.

12. Do the same thing with leg B.

13. Now put both paper clips on the drill cup hook and reverse spin the two legs together, furling them into one line. You want to reverse it until you get back the maximum length.

## finishing the furled line

If you want, you can just tie monofilament to the tippet end of the line and put a Dacron-backing loop through the loops on the butt end, and go fish. But there is a more elegant looking solution, called a Shorb loop. It isn't very hard and gives a nice, finished look that is secure by itself without any backing or mono added.

A Shorb loop is made by using a knit picker, which is found at any sewing store and used to pull snagged yarns back inside a sweater. Simply take the knit picker and go between the two leg cords of your furled line, a little more than a finger width from the end, and grab the end loops (from off of the paper clips) and pull through.

Now push the loops in the knit picker jaw that you grabbed from the paper clip and push them further down the neck of the knit picker. Lastly grab the lasso loop you just formed with the knit picker jaw and pull it through the loops. You're done. You have essentially pulled a loop (the lasso) through the strands behind the terminal loops you threaded down the standing line, securing it.

Pull hard on the loop to neaten it up. Do the same at the opposite end and you have a nicely formed loop on each end that can be used in a loop-to-loop connection.

I like putting a piece of backing that is tied in an overhand loop through the Shorb loop, joining them in a loop-to-loop fashion. This readies the line for a girth hitch to the lilian of your tenkara rod.

To the Shorb loop you can add a tippet ring or simply stick with a loop-to-loop connection. To put on the ring, tie it in with a short piece of stiff mono, a uni knot on each end. Stiff mono helps prevent tangles when you are fishing. You can also feed the tippet ring onto the furled line itself. I then feed the whole line through the tip loop, forming a knuckle around the tippet ring.

Of course you can vary the number of loops in a leg to change the taper and adjust casting characteristics. It is even possible to change thread color by tying in loops during the winding. These small knots are hardly noticeable and don't affect strength much in my view. I have seen both camouflaged and brighter indicator lines made this way.

If you want to give furling lines a try, 6-0 fly-tying thread (denier 135-140), or invisible nylon thread works well. These have been my best so far. Monofilament in #2 test works too, though you want to decrease the number of loops to avoid bulk. Very fine furled lines can be made with 8-0 thread, and some use fluorocarbon for a very dense line.

You can get pretty creative with furled lines. In my opinion there is no softer presentation than that produced by a furled line on a tenkara rod. Lately, I have been using shorter furled lines on my old Orvis too. (By simply using fewer pegs, the furling rig adapts to shorter lines.) Some tenkara anglers are even constructing traditional horsehair lines.

It's funny how some of the old ideas, like furled lines, occasionally come back into style.

### fluorocarbon lines/lines

You can spend a lifetime adjusting single filament lines, and plenty of western fly anglers do just that, designing taper to suit their own casting stroke and various fishing conditions. In keeping to tenkara simplicity, I will share just three "formulas" that illustrate three different approaches to building a tenkara single filament line. Each has its pros and cons.

When considering whether to fish single filament or furled lines, remember that fluorocarbon can be adjusted to length with a nipper, right on the water. Furthermore, they have more density and so can fight wind better than furled lines. Lastly they are easier to make. An angler simply joins sections of fluorocarbon (and nylon) together for a taper, or cuts the required length for a level line.

Dr. Ishigaki is perhaps the foremost level-line promoter in the world. He uses a yellow fluorocarbon line in either fourteen- or eighteen-pound test to which he adds tippet. He varies the length of the line, using everything from a line that's shorter than the length of his rod to one that's twice its length. The level line can be adjusted while he fishes. Inexpensive and simple, there is only one knot, the tippet knot, extending from rod to tip. If you want simple, this is the rig. I have found that ten-pound fluorocarbon can be effectively fished, providing added delicacy, though it is not as easy, nor as wind resistant. Heavier fluorocarbon is easier to cast. I've settled on fifteen-pound test for most of my level lines. On very tight brushy streams, it can be helpful to fish a line smaller than the rod length.

Misako fishes a slightly tapered line. She starts with a fluorocarbon line that varies from fifteen- to eighteen-pound test, depending on the wind and water conditions. This first section is generally the length of her rod, which is adjustable between thirteen and fifteen feet. To this she adds nylon monofilament for its better floatation. She uses a slightly smaller diameter length of monofilament, in lengths typically from one-quarter to one-half the rod length, followed by a small six-inch section of tinted

Amnesia indicator. She finally adds a very flexible tippet. As a competitive fly angler, she is used to efficiently fishing long lines. This is a great line for nymphing and wet flies, yet will work with dry flies too. At first you will find it a little unwieldy given that it requires an efficient cast to extend it fully. If you are having trouble, shorten the length of the nylon midsection.

I have been fishing a fully tapered fluorocarbon line lately. It is composed of four sections of fluorocarbon, each three feet, six inches long, in fifteen-, ten-, eight-, and six-pound fluorocarbon with an attached tippet ring. As is the case with western lines, by shortening the size of the butt and lengthening the midsections (from the traditional 60-20-20 Ritz rule of lines), you increase the delicacy of the presentation. Though I enjoy this very light throwing line, it limits my reach somewhat by its delicacy. Still it unrolls beautifully in a bow and arrow cast. My attempts to create longer tapers have been less successful in turning over a fly. Longer tapers must favor a longer and heavier butt section to lay out nicely.

Each of these approaches has its advantages. Heavier fluorocarbon transfers energy quickly, enabling a more accurate placement of the fly, and the use of heavier flies. It does add a bit of a "clunk" feel to the cast on super-light rods. Fluorocarbon is probably a better fit for boisterous and windy western waters. I like it on open water too, especially lakes.

A taper retains a degree of delicacy, allowing a fisherman to cast a smaller fly more softly. Tapers are for smaller water and delicate presentation.

If building a line with an indicator, consider taking the colored section you intend to use and making a French "sighter" or "slinky." Coil two feet or less of fifteen-pound tinted nylon monofilament around a bolt, securing it with wire or bread ties. Boil it for five minutes in water, then store it overnight in the freezer. The coil makes a very sensitive indicator for nymphing and is easily followed, though it does affect the cast. It is popular with competitive anglers.

As with so many things, there is no right answer and you may find a solution of your own. One thing all three of these approaches have in common is that fluorocarbon is necessary for efficient casting. The lack of stiffness and low density of nylon monofilament makes it a poor choice by itself.

Dr. Ishigaki: 13 to 31 feet of 14 to 18 Lb. fluorocarbon level line, tippet.

Misako: 13-15 feet of 15-18 Lb. fluoro, 3-7 feet of 12 Lb. nylon, 6 in. red nylon, tippet

Tapered: 3.5 feet each of 15,10, 8, and 6 Lb. fluorocarbon, tippet

When building a single filament line, I join each section simply with either double uni knots or double surgeon's knots, though a traditional barrel knot would be fine too. The double surgeon, a simple overhand knot with a second turn, is the best knot if the diameters of the two pieces are quite different. The knot can put a slight elbow at the junction compared to the other two, but I have not found this to be important in practice.

# CHAPTER 13

# tenkara backpacking

NOW I SEE THE SECRET OF MAKING THE BEST PERSON, IT IS TO GROW
IN THE OPEN AIR AND TO EAT AND SLEEP WITH THE EARTH.

—Walt Whitman

With tenkara rods telescoping down to sixteen inches and weighing as little as two-and-a-half ounces, a backpacker can take fishing gear without weight penalty, doubling their fun in the backcountry.

Having been a backpacker all my life, it is clear to me that fine-tuning your equipment is a continuous and important aspect of the sport. When carrying everything you need on your back, not only does the gear have to be reliable, but you need to consider the utility of what you carry. A good backpacking trip boils life down to its bare essentials. Every ounce becomes a burden that can affect the distance you cover and your comfort while doing so.

These past few years have seen a transformation in commercially available camping gear. The advent of ultralight camping has spawned a new industry of lightweight packs, shelters, and cooking gear. Indeed every aspect of backpacking equipment is being scrutinized for its weight and utility.[1]

Over the years, prior to tenkara, I was able to whittle down my fly-fishing outfit to a five-piece fly rod (breaking down to twenty-three inches), a four-ounce reel, and associated gear and gizmos, bringing my total, angling-gear weight to just under a pound. My tenkara rod with gear, however, comes in at an amazing six ounces! For the backpacker, tenkara is a revolution.

Moreover, given that my gear is much simpler and more accessible, I am more likely to fish. My five-piece required first putting the rod and reel together, then rigging the line through guides, and finally tying on a fly. It certainly was never at the ready. My tenkara rod can be stored fully rigged, including a fly, which allows me to fish spots that I would have previously passed up due to the inconvenience of rigging. I have even fished with my pack still on, something I had never done in the past.

Tenkara fishing is a perfect fit for backpacking. Its accessibility, storage, and utility will certainly appeal to the backpacker who scrutinizes and tweaks his or her gear toward efficiency and reliability.

## packing

Having your rod well protected but accessible is important, especially when crashing through chest-high brush, rock hopping, and scrambling across scree. I like keeping my rod in a lightweight plastic tube under the tightened side straps of my backpack. About five years ago I purchased a box of shipping tubes for four dollars. The tubes are closed on one end and have a screw top on the other. To the tube I attached a small piece of cord, which I tie to my pack as added insurance. I have also seen rods packed in the cellulose acetate tubing used for storing fluorescent lightbulbs. This is very lightweight and usually comes with end caps. If you are a real ultralight fanatic, packing your tenkara rod without a case at all will still likely work, as the rod handle is, in fact, a serviceable case.

My setup allows me to store the rod fully rigged, however, which in turn lets me take advantage of impromptu decisions to fish a little pool while I'm hiking. I wind my line and rigged fly around a cast winder of foam core stored with the rod inside the tubing. I can pull the fully rigged rod out and fish in seconds. If I know I won't be fishing during a walk (for instance, hiking the length of a ridge), I add one more layer of protection by storing the rod tube inside my tent pole pouch.

Using a packing tube also allows me to lash my packing tube to my trekking pole with a simple shear lashing as an alternative or when hiking to a stream from base camps. I start with a clove hitch on the trekking pole, wrap both with at least five wraps of small diameter cordage, then frap (a winding between the tube and pole that serves to tighten the cord wrappings) between the two, three or more times, ending with another clove hitch. (If that's not clear, ask any Boy Scout to show you a shear lashing.) This allows me to carry my rod close at hand completely rigged and does not interfere with the use of the trekking pole.

In camp, it is a good idea to keep your rod in its protective tube, safe from missteps. My packing tube has a small bottom vent for drying, and the attached slip of cord can be used to hang it from a branch stub. I've also written my name and cellphone number on the case with permanent marker.

Pack rafters will be interested in the experiences of Ryan Jordan, the ultralight backpacking author. In addition to using, endorsing, and selling tenkara rods, Ryan has had success storing his tenkara rod inside the paddle shafts of his pack raft, a nicely protected spot.

If you carry a small chest pack or fanny pack for fishing, a very accessible and secure place to carry it is simply belted around your pack. Clip it under the pack's hood straps for added security.

## camp fishing

With your rod rigged and at hand, a hiker can easily fish for a few minutes while his friends take a streamside lunch break. With tenkara you can fish your way into a campsite rather than first dropping your gear and then going back out to fish. Tenkara allows you to fish later into the evening too. If I'm fishing tenkara, I don't need to worry about navigating back to camp in the semi-dark with a rigged rod or breaking down my gear at streamside and risking lost sections. Tenkara rods can quickly be collapsed for easy navigation during night travel or bushwhacking, and sections remain secure.

As mentioned, tenkara rods are ideally suited to the waters encountered while backpacking. Many of these smaller streams and headwaters are often shadowed by brush and limb. Tenkara rods can more easily bow-and-arrow cast or tip flicked into tight spots. And while most anglers unfamiliar with tenkara are worried that their rod length makes them unsuitable for these tight streams, the tenkara rod can be partially collapsed for really tough spots (though your grip should move forward to the extended sections). Given the light weight, I will carry a tenkara rod even when I am not sure I will find fishable water, often discovering a beaver pond or stream worth a cast or two.

If you're planning an extended fishing trip into the backcountry, considerable thought should be given to your wading gear. Some wading boots are not all that heavy and can be tied to the outside of a pack when wet. They assure good footing but require putting on a damp shoe every morning (unless you want to risk drying them beside a campfire).

Neoprene fishing booties, like flats shoes or diving boots, don't really offer enough support or foot protection. Rocky stream bottoms can become pretty uncomfortable. And changing shoes means you have to carry or stash your hiking boots while you fish, and the latter option means a backtrack.

While fishing in your hiking boots is okay with some, I don't like walking in wet boots and I think the water takes a toll on the life of the boot. Furthermore, rock hopping along streams really restricts access to fishable waters, especially in wilderness areas with no trails.

Some fishermen favor Crocs, but I find that they can pull off easily in mud. Sandals have similar problems unless designed for wading, and usually have little toe protection. And both of these options make for cold wading in alpine waters and mountain streams.

My favorite wading gear is the NEOS River Trekker. Made with durable denier nylon, covering nearly the full leg, and with a rubber cleat sole, they pull on right over your hiking boot, giving great support in the water and allowing for a more comfortable hike in. They are decent rain pants, can crash through the brush without tearing, and add an effective layer in snow too. Comfortable enough for all-day wear, these hippers offer a quick place to put the butt of your rod when needing both hands. I often stuff my raincoat down my trekker leg, too. While they add about a pound to my load, I find the additional weight worth the sacrifice.

## campfire cookery

In accordance with the philosophy of ultralight backpacking (and thus, in the spirit of tenkara), I often like to supplement my meals with the fish I catch along the trail. (In heavily fished water or tender ecosystems, of course, I practice catch and release only.)

Generally I will try to catch middle-sized trout for supper, dispatching the fish with firm raps at the base of their heads (harder than you think), followed by opening them from vent to throat with a sharp knife. I remove the viscera and then scrape the bloodlines from the spines. (I like to drop waste back into the stream, where the entrails will be quickly recycled—this also helps avoid attracting bears.) A field stringer is as simple as a forked-stick passed through the gills.

I will almost always cook the fish whole, either on a green stick spit or directly in the fire coals. Pan-frying breaded trout requires hot oil and a cast iron skillet, fine for canoe camping but necessitating too much gear for backpacking.

Since trout will cook to easily flaked flesh in ten minutes or so, no more than a twig fire is generally needed for a couple of fish. I like to carry seasonings (salt, pepper, lemon salt, garlic, True Lemon, or seafood seasoning) in a screw-top plastic test tube of the type used for water testing. Onion grass, ramps (wild leeks), and sage can be added from the local flora too. Season the fish inside and out.

When using foil, leave some room when you seal it. You don't want it airtight around the fish. (If done carefully you can burn off the fish's remains and reuse the foil.) Coating the fish with oil or butter is helpful but not necessary. Be very careful to use only a reliably sealed container for any cooking oil you carry in your pack.

If cooking on a spit, sharpen a green stick with a fork in the smaller end. Thread the larger end from the body cavity through the mouth. You'll need to leave about four or five inches of stick exposed. Then force one leg of the forked stick through the body cavity and out the tail so that the fork holds and hangs the fish. After rubbing liberally with coarse salt, force the big end of the stick into the ground of the fireplace under the coals, vertically (tail up). Scoop more coals around the fish.

Cowboy style is the easiest. Simply lay the fish in the coals, turning once. The skin should be charred well when ready. I wait till after cooking cowboy style to add seasoning, if at all. This style of cooking gives the fish a bit of a smoked flavor.

To remove the bones, simply remove the flesh with a fork or knife working down from the backbone. When one side is gently fed off the bone, separate the ribs and spine by lifting the entire tail and spine while using a fork to tease the flesh loose. This is easier than it sounds, and almost always the remaining ribs and spine can be removed in one piece.

Poaching trout is another, surprisingly easy way to cook fish. Cut the trout into pieces small enough to fit into the pot, adding the chunks to boiling water a piece at a time. The cooked flesh falls easily from the bone and skin.

Relish and mayonnaise packets can turn leftovers into trout salad. Add some raisins too. Rolled up in pita bread, this makes a great streamside lunch. Taco seasoning with some cheese packets and a shredded carrot is an alternative.

A trout chowder can be made with just a few ingredients too. Simmer two packs of shrimp-flavored noodles and one pack each of dehydrated corn and peas and cook until soft, then simply add cooked trout. Garlic powder and Tabasco sauce are optional but sure add some zing.

The ultralight tenkara rod makes an ideal backpacking rod. Along with a couple flies and a spool of tippet, there is never a reason to leave it behind. No matter whether you're taking a day hike, or geared up for a week in the mountains, a tenkara rod adds to the adventure. It offers an entirely different approach to nature. Relying on your fishing skills to supplement your food supply adds seriousness to your sport. Preparing and cooking fish completes the circle of our food acquisition. Most of all, tenkara asks you to slow down and observe, with little interfering between the angler and his element.

---

## Sources from Pages 121-27

1. See www.backpackinglight.com.

風抜けて
落ち葉追いつく
濡れ毛針

石村美佐子 [印]

*misako*

# tenkara women

DOUBT NOT BUT ANGLING WILL PROVE TO BE SO PLEASANT, THAT IT
WILL PROVE TO BE LIKE VIRTUE, A REWARD UNTO ITSELF.

—Izaak Walton

"Women are naturally suited to fly fishing," says legendary fly fisher
and teacher Joan Wulff. Tenkara in particular is a match because of its
ultralight weight and reach.

Tenkara fly fishing will appeal to women for the same reasons it
appeals to men. It is a direct experience of the water, is inexpensive, and
can be learned with a minimum of fuss even while taking a lifetime to
master. Simplified by several centuries of production anglers, tenkara has
none of the rattle of the extraneous. It is straightforward without jargon
or specialization.

But tenkara has something more. Perhaps it's the grace of the tenkara rod, the tender flex that inscribes a nautilus curve, or that tenkara
has none of the crank and plop of spin-casting. Casting instructors often
admit that women are more naturally attuned to the rhythms of casting
efficiency and presentation than men. Misako, who trained in traditional
Japanese dance and then performed internationally, will be quick to note
that her fly fishing has been a natural progression of her study of rhythm
and grace. Beautiful and accurate casting does not come from power.
Tenkara casting is about controlled movement and good timing. Perhaps
this is why female anglers often understand the cast more quickly.

The many directions from which women come to fly fishing reflect
their diversity. Some have taken the "if you can't beat them" path to
enjoying couple-time with fly-fishing husbands. Tenkara is a quick way
to join spouses on the stream with a minimum of gear and instruction,

even while catching fish the first time out. It has no intimidating learning curve. It's also an effective way of entering into friendly competition on your own terms, perhaps even presenting a partner with alternatives to his tried-and-true methods. And of course, tenkara is just plain fun.

Tenkara rods are light enough for children, too. Tenkara is simple yet contains all the essentials needed to learn fly fishing. Children intuitively take to it. And by starting children early, they will grow up caring for nature and learning the importance of good water quality. They will come to understand the interwoven ecology of trout, insects, plants, and streamside animals. The beautiful trout will capture their attention and spark their interest, and stalking fish along a trout stream is always an irresistible adventure. Childhood memories are the irreplaceable treasures of such family outings.

Fly fishing is rapidly becoming a focus of friendship and support among women. The International Women Fly Fishers for example, for which Misako is goodwill ambassador, in the interests of promoting and educating women in the sport, has joined a large number of women's fly-fishing clubs together. Their annual conference and outing has become a focus of many fly-fishing friendships. Two groups, "Casting for Recovery" and "Reel & Heal," support women facing cancer. Fly-fishing clubs provide a supportive and noncompetitive environment in which to learn and join fly fishing. Joining a club is the quickest way to mastery. And with tenkara advocates like Misako involved, clubs are likely to increase in importance.

Perhaps most important of all, tenkara is a lifelong activity that can be enjoyed in the company of friends and family. The cycle of the fly-fishing day ensures the pace and pauses of thoroughly enjoyable outings, with quiet and laughter in equal measure. The shared anticipation and planning, the excitement of discovery, the joy of the catch, the streamside lunch, and long talks to and from a stream: These are the ingredients for the deepest of lifelong friendships.

From the 1400s, when Dame Juliana Berners, likely the first fly-fishing author, wrote about the health benefits of fishing the quiet stream, to the present, in which over 20 percent of U.S. fly anglers are female, women have been part of the sport. Now women are certainly in the leading wave of tenkara trendsetters as well.

# CHAPTER 15

# final word

LET US FIRST BE AS SIMPLE AND WELL AS NATURE OURSELVES, DIS-
PEL THE CLOUDS WHICH HANG OVER OUR BROWS, AND TAKE UP A
LITTLE LIFE INTO OUR PORES.

—Henry David Thoreau

**Tenkara is mostly for small streams** and intimate waters: the moss-covered hollows, the cool spring creeks, and sunny beaver pond. It's the intimacy, unencumbered by excess gear and gadgetry, that takes us outside of ourselves. We need our quiet places, both internally and out in the world, and tenkara can help you find them.

Tenkara in the end is just fishing: a sport, a challenge, a form of play. Yet it is important because it requires us to venture out, slow down, and observe. If we give ourselves up to the pursuit, we will learn things about ourselves and our world we never imagined. As the Irish proverb says, "If you listen to the sound of the river close enough, you can hear trout." Tenkara simply helps us listen more closely.

# Index

overhand knot. *See also* knots,
25, 26, 27
overhead cast. *See also* casting,
57–59
in small streams, 73

**P**
packs, 20
Parachute Adams (fly), 38, 108
Partridge and Orange (fly), 108
perfection loop knot. *See also*
knots, 28
pocket water. *See also* streams,
small, 73, 82
points. *See* lakes
poppers. *See also* flies, 85, 109
Pragliola, Roberto, 65
prime lies. *See also* fish,
spotting, 39

**Q**
quiet, importance of, ix–x, 76

**R**
red-eyes (fish), 85
Red Squirrel (fly), 108
"Reel & Heal," 130
relaxation. *See* quiet,
importance of
reverse hackle fly. *See also* flies,
77, 103

drawing of, 102
early use of, 2
tying, 104–5
rivers, 82–85
casting in, 82
dry flies on, 84
float tubes on, 85
using nymphs, 82–84
rods. *See also* lines, viii–ix, 1–2,
3, 9–12
action of, 10
*ayu* rods, 2
backpacking with,
121–24, 126
casting, 42, 53–67
1950 description of, 5
development of long rod, 2
early bamboo, 1–2, 3
Euro nymphing with, 83–84
first description of *kebari*
rod, 4–5
flexibility of, 15
grips on, 9, 11
holding, 54
landing fish, 87, 89–91
in large waters, 82
rating of, 10
reach of, 41, 47
rigging, 25–34
subsurface fishing, 45, 47, 48
telescoping storage, 9, 10–11

**T**

tailwaters. *See also* streams,
  small, 69–70
    insects in, 93–94
*tamo* (net), 20
tapered lines. *See also*
  fluorocarbon lines, 117, 118, 119
*Tateyama Mountain Climbing
  Diary* (Sato), 5
*tegara* (yellow butterfly). *See
  also tenkara,* 5
*tengara. See tenkara*
tenkara. *See also* lines; rods,
  viii–x, 133
    appeal to women, 129–31
    and backpacking, 121–22
    casting, 53–67
    dry-fly casting, 41–42
    early descriptions of, 4–5
    gear for, 9–23
    interest in United States,
      6, 7
    international interest in, 7
    landing fish, 87, 89–91
    modern resurgence of, 5, 6
    origin of, 1–2, 3–4
    origins of name, 5, 37
    planning approach to fish,
      38–41
    quietness and simplicity of,
      ix, x, 76

subsurface fishing, 45–49
Tenkara USA, 6
tension-swing cast. *See also*
  casting, 63–64
terrestrial insects, 93
thread. *See* furled lines
threaders, 34
tippets. *See also* lines, viii, 12,
  15–18
    attaching to fly, 30–34
    attaching to line, 26–30
    landing fish, 89, 90, 91
    nylon or fluorocarbon, 15
    sink rate, 47
    sizes of, 15
    tippet ring, 29
    tying monofilament to for
      indicator, 50
T.L.T. casting *(Tecnica Lancio
  Totale). See also* casting, 65
Tokugawa shogun, 1
Total Casting Technique. *See*
  T.L.T. casting
trout, 85
    cooking, 125–26
    vision of, 73–74
    and water temperature, 70

**U**

*ugui* (fish), flies for, 2

underhand cast. *See also* casting, 63–64

uni knot. *See also* knots, 29, 116, 119

United States, *tenkara* in, 6

Usual (fly), 107

## V

vests, 19–20

vises, 105

## W

*wabi sabi* aesthetic, 42–43

wading gear, 124
    waders, 22

Wales, *tenkara* in, 7

Walton, Izaak, 2

water, bodies of. *See* streams, small; large waters

water striders, 98

weather, cold. *See* winter

western fly fishing, vii–viii, x
    casting, 53, 64–65
    learning curve of, vii, 12
    PVC line for rods, 14

wet flies. *See also* flies, 45–49, 108
    in mountain streams, 59

nymphs, 46–47
reverse hackle fly, 77
for small streams, 72, 75
Soft-Hackle wet flies, 47–48
streamers, 48–49
using indicators with, 49–51

winter
    clothes for, 23
    flies for, 108

women, and *tenkara,* 129–31

Woolly Buggers (fly), 108

Wotten, Davy, 30

Wulff, Joan, 6, 129

## X

X-caddis (fly), 108

## Y

*yabiki. See* bow and arrow cast

*yamame* (fish). *See also* trout, 4, 5

yarn, as indicator, 49

Yellow Comparadun (fly), 108

## Z

Zebra Midge Nymph (fly), 108

zebra mussels, 22

# About the Authors

Dr. Kevin Kelleher is a family physician in the Blue Ridge Mountains of Virginia and a national spokesman for free clinics. A lifelong backpacker, canoeist, and a locally recognized painter, he has been teaching tenkara since its introduction into the US and is a member of the Asiatic Society of Japan.

Misako Ishimura was born in Osaka, Japan, but now resides in the Ozark Mountains near the White River where she teaches fly-casting and tying. She has been captain of the Japanese FIPS-Mouche World Fly Fishing team since 2000 and was a charter director of the International Women Fly Fishers and is currently their goodwill ambassador. Her instructors have included Joan Wulff and Japanese tenkara master Dr. Hisao Ishigaki, and her coordination of the Catskill Fly Fishing Center and Museum exhibition "Made in Japan" helped introduce tenkara to the US.